The Broken Halo
of Hobe Lett

A Western Adventure

Jim Burnett

Previous Praise From William H. Joiner, Jr.

Having had the pleasure of being asked to write a foreword for other books from Jim—it was a thrill to be asked to do another one. Not only has Burnett turned in another great new Western—he did it so quickly. How he manages to keep turning out these hits… I'll never know. Thank you, Jim! You are making my day.

William H. Joiner, Jr. – Author of the bestselling "Morgan Porter" series and the multi-million page read "Legend of Jake Jackson."

Previous Praise From Paul L. Thompson

The book you are holding might be the best Burnett Western yet! This author has the gift when it comes to telling stories. Just check out the way he sets the scene. His descriptions make you feel like you're almost standing in the story. Wonderful work—from a wonderful author. Check it out!

Paul L. Thompson – Bestselling author of the "U.S. Marshal Shorty Thompson" western series.

Previous Praise from C. Wayne Winkle

Stories like this make it better for Western readers. Every story of this quality that comes out makes the whole genre better. I am proud to be associated with Jim Burnett—and hope all the people who are enjoying my current number one bestseller "The Searcher" will head on over to read this new adventure!

C. Wayne Winkle – Bestselling author of the number one hit "The Searcher" and several other Western adventures.

The Broken Halo of Hobe Lett

Albert grinned as he leaned against the bar beside the drunk cowpoke in the smoke-filled saloon in Dalhart, Texas, pelting him with questions, holding his attention while Hobe, his younger brother, slyly picked the man's pockets from the other side. By the time the cowboy finished his last sip of whiskey, he was missing all of his money—greenbacks as well as coins. Not only that, but his smoke makings and timepiece were no longer in his pockets either, although he was too intoxicated to notice. After thoroughly fleecing their victim, the Letts walked shamelessly toward the door. But they weren't leaving without a challenge.

Tiller "Mule" Townsend, the short, round-bellied bar dog and owner, had seen their dirty deed, and he called their hand as he stood between the thieving brothers and the double doors. His bold stand wasn't made out of virtue. Townsend became privy to what they were doing the first week the Letts were in town. In fact, two evenings prior, he demanded a cut from their takings. Albert told him to go soak his shirt. This night, however, Mule (known by that name mainly because of his stubborn temperament) decided that if he wasn't getting any of the spoils, neither were they.

Sadistically and confidently, the brothers smiled at Townsend as he confronted them about the drunk they had just hustled. Hobe chuckled. "We were taught that a man should be full of the Spirit, not the spirits." The Letts knew that the chubby whiskey pusher had little regard for the drunk and his plunder being taken. Fact is, they had seen Mule overcharge customers for drinks and smokes nightly,

1

especially those who would surely suffer from barrel fever the next day. His thievery was simply a different kind than theirs, but just as crooked.

Albert nodded in agreement to his brother's sacrilegious silliness and said, "It's a fool who lets liquor steal his brains and money." He gestured with his head. "That cowboy got what he deserved." Townsend bristled up, that is, until Albert leaned into him and whispered, "And Mule Townsend, reckon you're about to get what you deserve if you keep blocking that there door. Ain't you ever heard it's useless to kick against the goads?" Albert's hand dropped to his gun, causing Mule to rethink his stance. He quickly stepped aside.

Townsend, although a greedy cuss, wasn't a fool. He valued breathing too much to say any more to these young guns. The way the brothers wore their Colts low on their hips gave Townsend pause. However, he wasn't so slow in putting other men's lives in danger.

As the brothers exited, Townsend immediately climbed on a chair and waved his hand, demanding his patrons' attention. "Two thieves just stole that feller's poke." He pointed to the drunk cowboy, who was now slouched at a table, passed out. His speech was incendiary and very persuasive, for thirty seconds later, six angry drovers pushed through the double doors, into the street, with pistols drawn and slurred profanity leaking from their mouths. Two of them held piggin' strings. They aimed to hog-tie the varmints who had cheated their partner out of his hard-earned wages and hang them by their feet. But they were no match for the fast guns of the Lett brothers.

"You fellers huntin' us?" yelled Hobe as he and Albert stepped from the shadows, fanning their guns and shooting out the flaming coal oil lamps hanging on both sides of the saloon doors. The drovers bottlenecked at the door as they pushed, shoved, and fell back inside, hunting cover and piling on top of each other like fallen dominoes. Within seconds, the swinging doors leading in and out of the establishment looked more like sieves than doors, riddled with bullet holes, all fired from the Letts' Colts. Not a single shot was returned from inside. The zip and zing of flying lead was enough to keep those on the floor from taking any further action, except for wetting their pants and cussing as they snaked across the wooden floor away from the hail of gunfire. Tiller was hunkered down behind the bar, his usual place of retreat when danger threatened.

Albert and Hobe were quickly making a name for themselves, albeit not a good one. Overnight, they had gone from milk to redeye, and now their faces would begin to appear on wanted posters all across the West, not just for nibbling or petty thievery like they had committed this night, but much worse: bank and train robberies, horse stealing, and property damage, ironically, mainly to churches. The Missionaries, the moniker they assumed and earned, seemed to be on a mission indeed—a sinister one that would break the heart of their mother and undermine most of what their father had taught them about God. In a twisted way, in honor of their deceased pappy, who was a preacher, they sacrilegiously quoted Scripture before, during, or after their dastardly deeds. They truly felt they had God's favor on their crooked schemes and believed they were doing His work. However, the day Albert shot and killed a bank clerk changed everything.

But why were Albert and Hobe Lett so jo-fired set on being highwaymen? That was a question their mother had pondered a hundred times since her sons had left home and chosen their wayward profession. The direction they were headed would have them bellying through the brush and living among the willows the rest of their lives, trying to stay ahead of posses, bounty hunters, and frontier lawmen, not to mention the infamous Pinkertons.

***

Hobe was a beautiful child when born, according to his mother, with a full head of brown, curly hair. His skin was olive-colored and his eyes dark brown. A prettier baby had never graced the earth. That assessment came from his mother, Selah. The same was said of Moses by his mother, Jochebed. What woman thinks any differently of her newborn offspring?

Hobe Lett grew up in a minister's home where the Bible was read regularly, and church attendance was not an option but a mandate. A compliant child he was, never giving his parents a minute's worth of trouble. He knew much Scripture by memory and sang in the churches his father pastored. Hobe demonstrated a pleasant disposition toward others. He was kind, considerate, and tender toward the things of God. In fact, at age eleven, Hobe gave serious consideration to following in the footsteps of his father. However, a series of unfortunate events took place that made Hobe rethink his future career. A storm of conflict was brewing in his heart that reached full strength a couple of years later. His older brother, Albert, was caught in the same storm. Neither, unfortunately, would weather it well.

The Dark and Ugly Side of Religion

As a Methodist pastor, Dan Lett, Hobe's pa, served eight congregations in his thirty-year ministry tenure, never with a membership of over one hundred. Often, he served two simultaneously, traveling by horseback into remote areas. Consequently, the pastor and his family moved around often. Hobe resented these moves. It seemed that just when he made a friend or two, it was time to pack up and leave. What bothered him more than relocating, however, was the reason for the moves: a group of church members requesting a different minister. Often, this left Hobe's father feeling rejected and somewhat a failure. In fact, the whole family shared similar sentiments.

Of course, Pastor Dan would always put a smile on his face and remind them that God had called him into ministry, and relocations were part and parcel of serving the Lord. In fact, there was nothing Dan Lett would not do for his Lord or the churches he served. He dearly loved to see people come to faith in Christ and help them along in their spiritual growth, and he had helped many do both. This pastor derived much joy from leading his people and carrying out his pastoral calling. Expanding the kingdom of God was the priority of his life.

However, being a minister was far from all butterflies and waterfalls. Often it required the pastor and his family to make sacrifices—sometimes sacrifices Dan's family resented. The Letts never owned their own house. They lived in one owned by the church. Dan was never paid much in salary either, which sometimes caused financial hardships.

His children wore many hand-me-downs, and there were very few new pairs of shoes bought or worn around the Lett household. There were even times when Pastor Dan was given a couple of chickens, a bushel of butterbeans, or a few heads of cabbage instead of money for his services. Dan hankered to give his wife and children more, just like any man desired, but pastoring a church in his day often forbade anything beyond the basic necessities of life. Again, Dan would never complain. He loved his calling and faithfully fulfilled it, but there were days and times when the burden of pastoring overwhelmed him.

Most Mondays, Pastor Dan found himself sort of wrung out from the previous day's long hours. Sundays often involved fourteen to sixteen hours of preaching, listening with empathy and praying with a member who was hurting, meeting with church leaders, and a host of other duties that needed his attention. And of course, there was usually a Monday morning critic who stopped by to bend his ear over his message or something else that did not suit him. Dan had even given his critic a name—not out of meanness but for much needed levity—Monday Morning Marvin. Of course, he did not share that with anyone but his wife, Selah. When he did, they both would smile as Selah gently reprimanded her husband. "Now, Pastor Dan."

Each time, Dan would follow her chastisement with, "Sometimes you have to laugh to keep from crying."

Dan and Selah were not the only ones struggling under the weight of the pastorate. Far too often, Hobe and his two siblings saw the ugly side of religion, and ironically, it was from the actions and words of church members. Late at night, they often overheard their parents discussing the latest crisis plaguing their father's congregation. The heart pine walls had knot holes, and their conversations, unfortunately, leaked through the walls. Somebody seemed to always be unhappy and did not hesitate to let Pastor Dan know about it. A few even threatened to have him relocated if he didn't pander to their wishes. As quiet and discreet as Hobe's parents tried to be about the challenges with the church, there was no hiding the toll the ministry was taking on the health of both Dan and Selah.

Dan apparently had the same ailments of the young preacher-boy Timothy in the Bible—stomach problems. But he did not subscribe to Paul's remedy of a little wine. He had seen too many of the ill effects of alcohol use in the towns and cities where he served, and Dan was resolved to abstain. Worse than his stomach ailments, however, were the chest pains and shortness of breath he experienced, which he kept from his congregation and family.

Selah, Hobe's mother, was not only worried about her husband's health, she was suffering from a hidden illness of her own—deep depression, which caused her to drift further and further away from people. Many times, Dan and the children saw Selah staring down at the floor with sadness. When they approached, she would change her expression to a smile. As hard as she tried, her sad emotions got the best of her.

Selah felt much guilt over her depression. *After all,* she told herself, *I'm a Christian and the wife of a pastor. My faith should be stronger than this. Why do I feel this way?* However, the reality was, she was a woman with a heart full of pain. And what pained her most was the cruelty of church people, especially toward her husband, who deeply loved God and the people of God. On Sundays, Selah saw the church people singing and praising the Lord, but the next day they were back to gossiping and backbiting. Too often, their favorite topic was her husband, Pastor Dan. Nothing hurt her

7

worse than to see the man she loved verbally attacked and demeaned. But her pain and depression only grew deeper when her children became the congregants' next targets.

An Unfortunate Dare

Albert Lett was Hobe's older brother. He bore the same name as his father, Dan Albert Lett, but that is where the similarities ended, according to the members of Grace Methodist Church in Casper, Wyoming. That was fine with Albert, because the last thing he wanted to be was a preacher, and many days, the son of one. He felt everyone was watching him and waiting for him to make a mistake. They didn't have to look hard or wait long.

Big brother Albert was an adventurous young man, fifteen years of age. He liked the city of Casper and the many things it had to offer. He enjoyed watching the expensive carriages, pulled by a pair of well-groomed, beautiful black horses, roll down Main Street. The drivers would drop off the wealthy, well-dressed Casper businessmen and their families at different places in town. Albert often wondered what it would be like to ride in such a carriage. Late one evening he found out.

He and his buddies were walking the boardwalks of Casper, when Grady Greer made a bold and daring challenge. He offered Albert and Caster Jacobs a pocketknife and six bits if they would take Mr. Theodore Lackey's funeral carriage for a drive. Albert hesitated. He knew this to be wrong, but riding in that big black, shiny carriage sure was tempting. At Caster's strong insistence and generous offer to drive, he acquiesced. Albert's poor judgment would be met with swift recourse, and to a degree, rightly so. They had taken a dead man for a ride in a stolen carriage. That was not only creepy, but criminal.

To climb into another's wagon and take the reins of his horses without permission was serious enough—a crime punishable by law. But hijacking a funeral carriage with a body in it was just too much for Mr. Theodore Lackey to forgive. Of course, the boys did not know that the corpse of old man Badger Jones was their cargo until they stood before the authorities and heard the cringing news.

Caster's father, Harry Jacobs, was a man of means. He owned a fabric store on Main Street and did a right smart of business. Mr. Lackey was offered one hundred dollars to forgive the trespass of Caster. He gladly accepted the money and gave a generous, full-throated pardon to the boy. "No harm done. Forgive and move on is my motto," said the undertaker.

Unfortunately, Albert's father, Pastor Dan, did not have one hundred dollars, and therefore Lackey was not so forgiving of Albert. Albert was required to perform three months of labor for the undertaker, although he was not the one who drove the carriage. His punishment, however, was far from over.

Dan spoke with Albert, and the boy regretted his foolish actions. He wished he had never taken Grady Greer's challenge. But as penitent as he was, his father required him to cut, stack, and deliver three cords of wood to some of the widow ladies in the community as well as the church's wood box. Hobe helped him fill the order. Unfortunately, Albert's chastisement fell short of some folks' expectations—mainly the members of his father's congregation.

The church leaders of Grace Methodist Church came calling at the Letts' house one Saturday evening. According to Pastor Dan, the most challenging things often happen on Saturday evening, just ahead of worship on Sunday. Dan even referred to it as the forces of the Devil at work to impede worship. The consensus of the men was that Albert should experience some form of public church discipline for his wrongdoing. They suggested he sit up front on the short bench for the next four Sundays. Dan wondered if their request was to discipline Albert or disgrace him. "And what do you require of the Jacobs boy?" asked Dan.

"We are not here to discuss Caster Jacobs, but Albert," one man said sternly. Caster Jacobs, who also attended the church, and who was the actual driver of Lackey's stolen carriage, was oddly not required to experience the same discipline as Albert. Some believed, especially the Letts, that was because Caster's father was a generous donor to the church, and the leaders did not want to risk upsetting his continued donations to the church's coffers. After all, five generations of Jacobs had attended Grace Methodist Church, and their names were handwritten on the inside covers of most of the hymnals, and engraved on the bottoms of all the offering plates, reminding folks of their faithful church support. Nobody, including the church leaders, mustered the nerve or possessed the conviction to suggest the young Caster Jacobs be disciplined. Not so when it came to the preacher's son, however. It was another bitter pill for the Letts to swallow, but swallow it they did.

The church leaders insisted that ministers' children should be held to a higher degree of accountability than other children in the church, and they believed that the discipline they recommended was appropriate and necessary. When Pastor Dan challenged the double standard, he was overruled. As the men left, Hobe watched his father slowly shut the door and turn to him with tears in his eyes. He would never forget this moment. The bitter winds were beginning to blow in this child's heart, and his teeth were set on edge.

Ironically, the first Sunday into Albert's detention, Caster Jacobs did something no one expected. He voluntarily joined his friend on the short bench, to the obvious displeasure of his father as reflected by the stern look on his face. Caster's conscience bothered him too much to let Albert take the blame by himself. But he was not the only one. Hobe, Selah, and Julie, Albert's sister, kept him company as well. Consequently, the short bench was packed, with no room for another unruly believer.

Hobe Lett was now getting a full dose of ugly religion at the hands of church people. His anger began to grow and take deep root in his heart. He was upset that Christians could be so cruel toward his brother. Unfortunately, the church's injustice would next be meted out on his sister.

Julie's Shame

Julie was a vivacious twelve-year-old who was on the bloom. She had beautiful jade-green eyes, a carefree spirit, and an infectious laugh. Julie loved to take walks down the road behind the church, singing as she went along. One day, as she frolicked alongside a creek bank that ran parallel with the road, she came across a stranger who was fishing. Julie waved and smiled at the man and continued on her way, humming a tune and skipping. But before she reached the road again, the stranger stepped in her path and brutally attacked her.

Later in the afternoon, Selah began to worry about her daughter and sent the boys to fetch her. Albert and Hobe found their sister where the stranger had left her—by the creek bank, in some willow saplings and cattails. Julie's clothes were torn, and her face was a mess. She was confused and crying. Her brothers got her home as quickly as possible, not fully comprehending what had happened.

Two months later, Julie experienced severe stomach pains and was taken to the family doctor in Casper. He confirmed Dan and Selah's greatest fear. Their twelve-year-old daughter was pregnant with child, through no fault of her own, of course.

Julie was devastated by this news, as was the rest of her family. She was ashamed of her condition, but her mother and father, as well as her brothers, showed her love and encouragement, as did several of the older, godly widow ladies in the church. Sadly, however, a majority of the leaders and most of the rest of the congregation, once again, failed to show mercy to the pastor and his family. They did the unthinkable.

As before, the church leaders came calling on Pastor Dan at the parsonage. Again, it was Saturday evening, and as Dan often said, very challenging things happened on Saturday evenings, ahead of worship on Sunday. The six men nervously entered the home, their eyes darting back and forth at one another as they stood inside the door. From the look on their faces, Dan knew it was going to be an unpleasant exchange, and so did Selah, who stood quietly in the kitchen, kneading dough, cutting up potatoes for supper, and praying. Albert and Hobe stayed outside on the porch, but even from there, they heard the cruel and hateful verdict.

All six of the church leaders expressed their sorrow over what had happened to Julie, but that was where the consensus ended. Four of the six said that in her condition, she should not come back to the church, and perhaps should even be sent away until after the baby was born. Of course, they assured Dan that this was not their opinion, and that they were only messengers of what the majority felt was appropriate. But as Dan knew, so often the majority was wrong, and this was one of those times.

Dan could not believe what he was hearing. He was a well-tempered man who always seemed to be able to hold his tongue and be patient, even when dealing with the worst of people. He remembered only a year before, when a young lady in the church, a relative of one of the men standing before him, had given birth to a child out of wedlock. She was not asked to leave Casper or the church. Yet, the men in his home who were forbidding his daughter from returning to church were the spiritual leaders of Grace Methodist Church, the examples for others to follow. How could this be?

Selah broke down and wept, and her wailing could be heard by everyone in and near the house—the church leaders and the rest of the family. Dan's face was wrinkled and reddened. His fists balled up. Only by the grace of God was he able to control his angry impulses. He simply walked to the door and asked the men to leave, and because of the look on his face, the church leaders exited quickly.

As they stepped out onto the porch, one of them walked by Albert and made the mistake of patting him on the shoulder. "Good to see you, son."

Albert pulled away in contempt. Hobe snorted and shook his head, disgusted beyond words. Dan pushed open the screen door and quickly called the boys into the house. He knew they were angry, and if pressed, they would lash out at the men, maybe even taking a swing at them. Albert and Hobe obeyed their pa, but it did not abate their fury. They sneered at the church leaders as they walked by them. Dark clouds were gathering over these brothers, and a terrible storm was on the way.

From her bedroom, Julie had overheard the conversation between her father and the church leaders, and later that evening, she pleaded over and over with her parents to let her leave Casper and go stay with Selah's sister and her husband in Kimmerer, Wyoming. Sad and feeling rejected, she did not want to attend a church where she was not welcome. After two weeks of her incessant pleas, Dan and Selah reluctantly granted her request. With great sadness, they packed her up and sent her by train to her aunt and uncle's. Albert and Hobe were livid. Once again, the Lett family had drunk from the cup of ugly, godless religion. This time, however, the cupful would be too much for Dan to swallow.

Jim Burnett

Early Retirement

Seven months after Julie's forced relocation, just hours before her baby's birth, Dan Lett suffered a fatal heart attack. He was forty-eight years old. His family was devastated. But just what sent Pastor Dan to his early grave? Was there a family history of heart problems passed on to this man through his lineage? That did not seem likely, given Dan's father, Elvin, was in his late seventies and still a man of vigor. To boot, Elvin's father, Ruel, Dan's grandfather, lived to be ninety-two. So, what caused Dan to die prematurely, well shy of the three score and ten years the Bible predicts for man? The doctor diagnosed it as stress, tension, and worry. Dan's family believed it to be a broken heart.

No man ever loved God, his family, or church more than Dan Lett. He gave his heart and soul to all three. But when Julie, his precious daughter, his pride and joy, his little girl, was cruelly sent off in shame, it was too much for Dan to stomach, and obviously, too much for his heart to endure.

Hours before he died, he reminisced to Selah about Julie's way of lighting up a room with her smile. Many times, when he was worried about something or in a bit of a somber mood, his little princess would come sit in his lap, and with a big crooked grin, she would tell her dad she loved him. For that moment, his cares vanished. He also told Selah how much he missed the innocent and childlike way in which Julie saw life. She always saw the good in others and spoke pleasantly of everyone. To Julie's credit, she never even spoke a harsh word about her attacker, but she did pray for him.

In the last few minutes of Dan's life, just before crossing into the heavenly realm, this man of God saw five angels

17

hovering over his bed, and he spoke of their beauty. A big smile came over his face as he looked up. Then he looked around the room and spoke of things he regretted. He cried about his failure to protect his daughter from that terrible attack at the pond. He lamented not rebuking the church leaders and their cruel insistence that his daughter be whisked away, out of town and out of sight, because of her pregnancy. "Please tell Julie that I love her and ask her to forgive me. Give her the letter that's in my Bible."

"I will, my love," said Selah. "I will."

Dan knew he was about to fly away and wanted to get his house and relationships in order. "Albert, I'm sorry, son, for allowing the church to make you sit on the short bench. That was not right of me. I'm sorry. I should have put those church leaders on the short bench." Albert laughed, as did Hobe. "I'm sorry, son." Dan put out his hand.

"It's okay, Pa," Albert said, tears streaming down his face as he leaned over and hugged his father.

"Hobe," Dan called out.

"Here I am, Pa."

"Listen to the voice of God, son. Don't be angry with church folks or let bitterness take root and ruin your life. Use your beautiful tenor voice for the Lord. You've blessed so many with your singing." Dan had seen Hobe's tender heart for God change in the last year, and as a Christian father, he was concerned about him. There seemed to be a sleepless hate growing in Hobe's soul, and in Albert's as well. "You boys are my pride and joy. Stand strong. Take care of your ma and your sister and that little baby who's coming." Dan smiled. "I'll see you on the other side." They both fell on his chest and wept. Dan stroked their heads. "Don't cry for me, boys, Heaven is before me, and the Lord is calling."

In Dan's final moments, he took Selah by the hand and expressed his remorse for not being able to help his wife with her deep bouts of sadness. He told her he was sorry that her life had been so hard. His dying words were, "Forgive me, my precious family, Selah, Albert, and Hobe, for failing you." He took one final breath and whispered, "I love you." His spirit left his body and entered the presence of God. Dan's retirement had come early. His ministry had been hard, but now, in the presence of Jesus, he was enjoying the fruits of his labor.

At Dan's funeral, the entire congregation of Grace Methodist Church turned out, as well as many other residents of Casper who did not attend the church, but who respected this man of God. The Letts stood next to Dan's casket as people funneled by, expressing their sympathy with words and hugs. Selah had spoken with her three children before Dan's service began and encouraged them, out of respect for their father, to refrain from any negative words or gestures toward anyone. They honored their mother's wishes. Julie, with her newborn baby Danielle, named after her pa, stood next to her mother as the ladies came by and told her what a beautiful little girl she had. It was almost more than Albert and Hobe could stomach. It was like chewing on bitter weed with nowhere to spit. These were the same folks who had banished their sister as if she was an outlaw, just because of her pregnancy out of wedlock—a result of rape.

Reverend Elvin Lett, Dan's father, preached his son's funeral. He broke down several times and could not speak, deeply grieved over the premature death of his son. But he knew exactly where his boy was—in the presence of the Lord. After the service, the family, along with the church members, went out back to the graveyard and laid Dan to rest. Two men stepped forward at the graveside and spoke of Dan's godly character and how he had helped them. If only people would have given Dan his flowers while he was alive. But like so many do, they waited until his death.

After their words, Reverend Lett said, "Into thy hands we commit Dan to you, Lord." Selah bent down, just before the men with shovels covered his grave, and picked up a handful of dirt, tossing it atop her husband's casket. Her children did likewise. When the three men began shoveling the dirt into the six-by-six hole, Julie wept uncontrollably as she cradled Danielle against her chest. Albert took his niece into his arms while Selah and Hobe put theirs around Julie. No amount of dirt, or anything else for that matter, could fill the gaping hole in the hearts of Albert and Hobe Lett, unless of course it was the thought of revenge and retaliation toward religious folks. The brothers knew, however, this was not the time nor the place for either, so they swallowed their feelings and got through the day.

These boys had seen their share of ugly, hollow religion. It wasn't just their father who endured harsh remarks from parishioners and constant accusations that every problem in the church was linked to his incompetence or inadequate leadership. Selah, their mother, the pastor's wife, at times felt so lonely, so left out. Many times, church ladies had quiltings, tea parties, and baby and wedding showers or other social get-togethers. Yet, they never seemed to want to include Selah, mainly because she was the pastor's wife. Selah rarely said anything to Dan or her children as to how this made her feel. She didn't have to; it was all over her face.

Dan encouraged Selah to reach out to a couple of the ladies in hopes of her developing friendships. On both occasions, the women she attempted to befriend did not reciprocate. Consequently, Selah, feeling dejected and unwanted, withdrew into herself. She went to church and supported her husband, but she had nobody she could confide in or call a friend.

Then, talk began among church members that the pastor's wife seemed unfriendly, aloof, and unwilling to participate in church activities. In the parishioners' minds, the pastor's wife was just simply not doing all they thought she should be doing. This only added to Selah's feelings of isolation and condemnation. Dan often told Selah to ignore the expectations of others. He was grateful for her support of his ministry, but more importantly, for being the love of his life. Always, she was his chief supporter and encourager, constantly understanding of his many hours away from home, caring for congregants and their crises. Nonetheless, Selah constantly apologized to Dan that she was a failure at measuring up to what a pastor's wife should be.

Dan often thought what a shame it was that the people of his congregation never really got to know the wonderful and precious lady Selah was. The title of pastor's wife blinded them to who she was as a person—a warm, caring, lady, full of grace and mercy. Yet, they really never gave her a chance to be herself because they were too predisposed to what a pastor's wife ought to be and do.

As sad as it was that Dan was gone, at least now the Lett family felt they could move out of the glass house in which they had been living and just be ordinary people. Within two weeks of Dan's funeral, the family moved from Casper, Wyoming to Garden City, Kansas. They wanted a fresh start.

Jim Burnett

The Early Days of The Missionaries

Albert and Hobe helped their mother, sister, and their newborn niece, Danielle, get settled with their grandparents in Garden City. The boys worked some odd jobs around town to support their mother and Julie. However, their plans were to set out as soon as they raised enough money to travel. These brothers, who would soon become known as "The Missionaries," were about to ride across the frontier, bringing a twisted kind of justice to humanity, especially those who called themselves Christians yet showed only rotten fruit.

Albert was eighteen, and Hobe was sixteen when their outlaw days began. They left Garden City and struck for Cimarron. They each quickly found work. Albert swamped for the Salt Lick Saloon, and Hobe helped in Stokes' Mercantile. The Letts never disclosed to any of the townsfolk that they were brothers. They decided before coming to Cimarron that it would be in their best interest to keep that fact to themselves.

With Albert working in the saloon on one side of the street, and Hobe working the mercantile on the other, it wasn't long before the two of them got the skinny on the town. The more men drank, the looser their tongues became, and Albert was there to gladly steal their secrets, and often, their money.

There was no shortage of gossip from the ladies who visited the mercantile either. Mrs. Bonnie May Stokes, who owned the store with her husband, Joe, was an incessant gossip who would rather spend her time spreading rumors than selling goods. Hobe stocked the shelves, swept the floors, and listened, with great interest, through the grapevine of these women. It wasn't long before Albert and Hobe determined who the hooking bulls of Cimarron were, and who was causing the most trouble in the town—specifically, in the church.

One night, after Albert locked up the saloon, he heard some drunken drovers in the side alley and decided to pay them a visit. Two of them were passed out, and the other lay on the ground, mumbling. Albert unhitched the gun belts of the two passed-out men and hid the coiled-up belts carrying Colts under his jacket. When he reached his room on the second floor of Molly Grimmick's boarding house, he lit a lamp on the table and laid out the guns on the bed. He and Hobe had been saving up to buy pistols, but now there was no need.

Hobe walked into the room to find his brother sporting an 1851 model Colt on his hip. With his mouth gaped open, he pointed at the gun. "Albert, where in tarnation did you get that shootin' iron?"

Albert grinned. "In the alley out back. Those fellers lying on the ground didn't look like they were using them."

Hobe brushed his brother's shoulder with his hand. "That's a fine pistol you got there, Albert. Reckon I'd like one myself."

"Well, little brother, ask and you shall receive. Isn't that what the Good Book says?" Albert gestured at the other gun and belt on the bed. "That one there is yours." It was also an 1851 Navy Colt.

The Lett brothers were beside themselves as they stood before the mirror in their room, provisioned with side arms, grinning from ear to ear, and practicing their draw and dry firing. Now they had to learn to use the weapons, which would not take these fast learners long.

Albert and Hobe joined up at a washed-out gully outside of town every afternoon and practiced their drawing and shooting. Within weeks, these brothers could hit anything they aimed their irons at. The only thing more impressive than their accuracy was the speed at which they could draw. These two skills, coupled together, made these boys a dangerous, deadly duo.

Now that they had their marksmanship down, it was time to do what they had come to town to do. Cimarron would be the first place The Missionaries would introduce themselves and carry out the first of their many deviant missions. They fully intended to vindicate their father, even though it would prove to be in a very twisted manner.

Albert and Hobe had been attending a small community church in Cimarron for several weeks. They had gotten close to the pastor and his family and shared several meals with them at the parsonage. These brothers had determined that Pastor David Touchstone and his family deserved more than shabby clothes, a rundown shack, and a worn-out carriage. These boys did not subscribe to the theory about men of the cloth that some folks in Cimarron seemed to believe: *Lord, you keep them humble, and we'll keep them broke.* The Lett brothers thought a man of God, a person who had surrendered himself to do the Lord's will, to take care of the Lord's people, to go wherever and whenever there was a need, should be rewarded. After all, these boys said to one another, an ox should not be muzzled when it is working, and a workman is worthy of his wages.

Pastor Touchstone and his wife, Trudy, were impressed with the Lett brothers' grasp of the Scriptures. Week by week, they grew closer and closer to these young men. Even the Touchstones' three children shared a special bond with Albert and Hobe. In fact, one of the Touchstone children was named Julie, the same as their sister. That endeared her even more to the Lett brothers.

But it was now time for the Lett brothers to go. However, they would not leave until they righted the wrongs they saw in Cimarron. Albert had witnessed Burt Nettles, the owner of the Salt Lick Saloon, abusing several of the saloon girls and also cheating those who were gambling in his establishment, not to mention that he berated him, many times, in front of the customers—shoving him around and yelling obscenities. Albert devised a plan to bring the big-bellied, big-mouthed Nettles to heel. He would hit him where it hurt the most—in his money belt. Nettles always wore it inside his shirt. Before it was over, Albert planned to break the saloon owner's habit of assaulting and berating his employees.

Lily, a fair-skinned, young, skinny saloon girl with wavy blond hair, told Albert that Nettles was cheating people at blackjack and at the roulette table. One evening, Albert and Hobe enlisted the help of two gamblers who had just arrived by stage to help clean Nettles' plow. The four of them agreed to split the earnings after Nettles' scam was exposed. The plan worked beautifully. That night, the visiting gamblers waited until there was big money on the table to lay bare the fraud. Consequently, they left with their pockets bulging with money, and the cheaters were hauled off to jail. Later that night, Albert and Hobe visited the gamblers' rooms for their cut. The Letts pocketed over six hundred dollars.

The next night, Albert arrived for work, and Nettles was in a foul mood. He threw glasses across the room, kicked chairs, and turned over tables. Anyone who looked at him wrong received his full wrath. "I want to know who ratted on me, and I want to know, now!" He slammed down his fist on the only table that remained standing.

Unbeknownst to Nettles, Albert had come to work toting iron under his apron, figuring he'd need it for defense if the big man took a swing at him. Nettles stomped around the place like a bull in a china shop. He made all his employees line up against the bar where he began interrogating them one by one.

When he got to Lily, Albert knew this young, very nervous girl would probably sing, so he stepped forward and addressed Nettles. "Boss, figure I know who finked on you. Can we talk out back? These walls have ears."

"All right, Lett. Rattle your hocks and follow me," barked Nettles. "I want to know the dead man who's responsible for my losses."

When Albert walked by Lily he winked, relieving her of any fear of being found out by her boss. Then he went through the door leading out back where he found Nettles fuming mad. "All right, boy, who's the skunk that—"

Before he could finish his question, Albert shoved his Colt in Nettles' face. "Hobble your jaw, fat man, and listen."

Nettles was dumbfounded. He didn't even know Albert owned a gun, much less that he possessed the courage to use it. "You better—"

Albert creased the big man's mouth with the barrel. "I thought I told you to stall your mug. You don't listen very well, but you'll learn."

Nettles quickly came to heel. This was an Albert Lett he had never met, and he knew it was always dangerous to meet a stranger and try to figure what he would do when push came to shove. So, the saloonkeeper stood at full attention and waited for Albert's next command. "Mr. Nettles, you've been weighed and found wanting in character. Your behavior is intolerable. You will never again raise your hand to a woman or your voice to any of your employees. Do you understand?"

Nettles nodded.

"A nod is not good enough, sir."

"I understand," grunted Nettles.

"Are you willing to take an oath on it?"

"Yes."

Albert slowly put his pistol into his holster. "Raise your right hand and speak your oath."

Nettles raised his hand and mumbled, "I won't hit another woman or yell at my employees."

"Now," said Albert, "keep your hand up because I want to make a pledge to you. I promise, if I hear that you hit a woman, yelled at a worker, or cheated at your gambling tables, I'll come back and shoot off another one of your fingers."

Nettles was puzzled at Albert's warning. He did not understand what he meant when he said he would shoot off *another* finger, that is, until he saw the flash and smoke from the young man's Colt and felt the pain in his hand. Nettles fell to his knees and grabbed the bloody nub on his right hand. Albert meticulously opened the loading gate on his pistol chamber and pulled out the spent cartridge, thumping it at Nettles contemptuously. His eyes darted back and forth from Nettles to his Colt as he slid in another round. He holstered his gun and slowly walked away, reciting Scripture. "A man reaps what he sows." Just before leaving the alley, Albert turned and gave Burt a final warning. Shaking his finger at him, he said, "Remember your oath, because I'm goin' to remember mine."

Across the street, Hobe was getting ready to administer his own brand of justice to Bonnie May Stokes. For weeks, he'd heard this woman gossiping about the folks of Cimarron. But what really got his goat were the multiple derogatory remarks she flung out about Pastor Touchstone and his family. As the son of a preacher, Hobe resented them. Bonnie May poked fun at the thread-worn clothes the pastor's children wore, and the hairstyle of Trudy, his wife. She also said Touchstone's sermons were much too long, and his shoes needed polishing. Her comments drew laughter from the store patrons, but Hobe was repulsed each time Bonnie spoke her cruel words. Today he was determined to give her a dose of her own medicine.

When Joe and Bonnie Stokes stepped out for lunch, Hobe decided it was time to implement his plan. The first step was doing a little gossiping of his own. But who would be his carrier pigeon?

The lunch crowd in the mercantile was small, but Hobe knew it only took one wagging tongue to start a wildfire in a town like Cimarron. Walking through the door was the perfect host for the gossip Hobe wanted spread—Mrs. Theodore Price, the mayor's wife, and president of the Women's Missionary Union of the church—the biggest blabbermouth in Kansas, at least in Cimarron, Kansas.

"Hello, Mrs. Price. How can I help you today?"

"Mr. Hobby," she said with a hint of condescension.

"It's Hobe, ma'am."

"Yes, well," Mrs. Price answered irritably. She didn't like that the young store clerk corrected her. "I need three spools of red thread and two needles."

"Will that be all, Mrs. Price?" Hobe asked as he bagged the items.

"Yes, that is all."

"Ma'am, have you heard Mrs. Bonnie's plans for Reverend Touchstone and his family?"

"Well, no, Hobby, I haven't." She threw her hand to her chest, embellishing surprise. "Do tell."

"It's Hobe, ma'am."

"Well, get on with it, Hobe," Mrs. Price said angrily. "Tell me what Bonnie May plans to do."

"Well, ma'am, I was told not to tell a soul, and I might lose my job if she finds out."

"Hobe, I demand you tell me right this minute."

At least now Mrs. Price knew his name, Hobe thought, but he knew he could no longer keep her on the hook. He waved her in as he leaned over the counter. Mrs. Price, starving for the breadcrumbs of gossip, quickly met him in the middle.

"You know how kind-hearted Mrs. Bonnie May is, and how she likes to keep her good deeds under cover, but I'm going to tell you anyway."

Mrs. Price nodded exuberantly and said, "Yes, yes, I know. Go on, Hobe." She didn't really consider Bonnie May that kind-hearted or all that modest, but her ears were itching for the dainty morsels of chinwag about to spill out of Hobe's mouth.

Hobe continued with a faint whisper that had Mrs. Price on her tiptoes, leaning over the counter. "I heard Mrs. Stokes was going to provision Pastor David with a new pair of shoes and a watch. Maybe that will help him shorten his sermons." Hobe chuckled. "Mrs. Trudy's gettin' a new dress, a brush, and some bows for her hair, and the children, new outfits, right out of the store window."

"You don't say!" said the mayor's wife.

"Well, ma'am, I would appreciate it if you didn't tell anybody what I told you. Let it be just between you and me." Hobe pointed his finger toward her and back to himself.

Mrs. Price rubbed her chin in deep thought. Hobe cleared his throat and said, "Mrs. Price, you're not going to tell anyone, are you? Mrs. Price?"

"Oh, Hobby, I won't tell a soul."

For the moment, Hobe Lett didn't care that the number one gossip in town, just slightly ahead of Bonnie May, of course, had again mispronounced his name. He knew what he had told her about Bonnie May's good intentions would be repeated with complete accuracy. And that was precisely his mission today.

In less than an hour, the store was filled with ladies who were intent on speaking with Mrs. Bonnie May. One by one they expressed regard for her generous intentions toward the pastor and his family.

"A new suit and watch for the reverend," said one of the ladies. "Why, that's just splendid, Mrs. Stokes."

Bonnie May was speechless and stood as if paralyzed. Some thought it was modesty on display, but in reality, she was struggling to process the rumors concerning her generosity. Another person mentioned the good deed of outfitting the minister's children with new clothes and shoes from right out of the storefront window. A third lady came in and told Bonnie May how proud she was to have a friend who showed such love and appreciation to the pastor's wife. If Bonnie herself wasn't surprised enough by all this news, Joe, her husband, made up the balance. With each good intention mentioned, Joe looked up to the ceiling and tallied up the cost in his head. When the final total came to his mind, he almost swallowed his quid of tobacco.

For the rest of the afternoon, people streamed in and out of the mercantile, each one impressed with the Stokes' generosity. When closing time came around, Joe quickly flipped over the sign on the front door and pulled down the shade. He turned and let out a loud sigh then lit into his wife. "Bonnie May Stokes, what in Sam Hill have you done? You've given away the store."

Mrs. Stokes was obviously frazzled. She plopped down on top of the cracker barrel and said, "Joe, I never... I don't understand."

Joe showed no empathy or sign that he believed her. "Do you know how much all those things will cost us? It will take twelve months to recoup that money."

"I know, Joe, but I'm telling you, I never said I was going to give the preacher and his family any of those things."

Hobe played the innocent. "So, the reverend is not going to get a new suit and watch, ma'am? And Mrs. Trudy and the girls—no new clothes and such? That's too bad, not only for the minister and his family, but what will the townsfolk think when you tell them? Reckon they'll be a little disappointed, huh?"

"He's right," said Bonnie May as she pointed at Hobe while looking at Joe. "We'll be the laughingstock of Cimarron. My good name will be ruined." Hobe gnawed on his lower lip to keep from showing his gratification. "Joe, please, we've got to give the pastor and his family the things the townsfolk say we promised."

Joe wagged his head back and forth and kicked a sack of flour, causing his face to pucker with pain. He turned and pointed at his wife. "Bonnie May, I declare, I don't know how this all happened, but I figure your gossiping ways have caught up with you—with us. Seems to me, I recollect you poking fun at the preacher's clothes, his long sermons, his wife's clothes, and their children's. Maybe the good Lord is teaching you a lesson."

"What would that be, Joe?" asked Bonnie innocently.

Without hesitation, he answered sternly, "To hush up, woman."

Hobe excused himself. As much as he was enjoying watching Mr. Stokes reprimand his wife, he didn't want them suspecting him of foul play. "If you don't need me anymore, Mr. and Mrs. Stokes, figure I'll call it a day." He waved and walked toward the back door. "See you tomorrow."

First thing the next morning, when the store opened, the Stokes sent Hobe to fetch the Touchstones—all five of them—and bring them to the store. Before the minister and his family left the store, they were given everything the people of Cimarron said the store owners had promised them. Not only that, when they returned to their home, a brand-new horse and buggy were at their hitching post, and there were toys for the children on the front porch. It wasn't Christmas, but to the Touchstone family, it sure felt like it. There was a note on the door that read, *Thank you, Pastor Touchstone, for all you and your family do for God and the people of Cimarron. We love you and appreciate you. Your grateful congregation.*

The Stokes had provided all the clothes, but who gave them the horse and buggy? It was Albert and Hobe. The night before, they had ridden to Garden City and bought the rig with the money they finagled from exposing Nettles' gambling practices. When Hobe escorted the Touchstones to the Stokes' mercantile, Albert drove their new transportation, along with two bags of toys, over to their house.

However, pride is a funny thing. Not to be outdone, Mayor Tom Price, at the strong recommendation and demand of his wife, declared this day in Cimarron as Pastor

David Touchtone Day. Pastor David was given the key to the town, and with it, a free professional haircut, a free dinner for his family of five at Chester's diner, and free milk and cheese for a month from the town's dairyman. He was also promised some updates to the parsonage. Within days, local carpenters installed a new front porch to replace the rotted out and dangerous one, a pump inside the house, which made things much easier on Trudy for cooking and cleaning, and a new roof on the lean-to for the parson's horse and rig. For an entire week, the people of Cimarron brought meals to the parsonage, expressing their thanks. It seemed everyone in town was intent on showing their appreciation to the Touchstone family.

Albert and Hobe struggled to keep straight faces as they watched the citizens of Cimarron, who just days ago, seemed to take their pastor and his family for granted, and now could not do enough for them. It certainly seemed that generosity begat generosity. It was time for The Missionaries to move on to their next mission. As they rode out of Cimarron, Albert said, "God sure loves a cheerful giver, huh, little brother?" Hobe grinned and nodded, and the boys gathered their reins, galloping away. It bothered them not that they had used deception, lies, and violence—all methods of the Devil—to right the wrongs of Cimarron. They were now on a dangerous path that would lead them further and further from God, yet all the while, in some way, they believed they were doing His will.

Jim Burnett

Shootout in Dalhart

Albert and Hobe put a lot of thought and planning into the places they planned to visit in order to carry out their twisted mission endeavors. The brothers were wise enough to put sufficient distance between the last town they bilked and the next, usually about two hundred miles or so. Therefore, after Cimarron, they decided to strike for Dalhart, Texas, which was located in the northwestern corner of the Texas panhandle. Crossing into the plains of Oklahoma, the brothers saw a lot of pheasants and jack rabbits, which made for some good meals cooked over their spit. Each day, they got closer to Dalhart. At night, Albert and Hobe sat around their campfire, sipped coffee, and plotted and planned their strategy for the Texas town.

When the boys arrived in Dalhart, one of them rode in from the east side of town, and the other from the west, about fifteen minutes apart. They both went into a diner, but they entered separately and sat at different tables. When they finished eating, they visited one of the saloons where they fleeced a local resident who was drunk. They stayed in Dalhart for two weeks. Each night they visited a different saloon, with the purpose of stealing from those who were intoxicated. There were four different saloons in town. Up to this point, the brothers had been highly successful working together. However, their luck was about to play out.

Tiller Townsend, one of the Dalhart barkeeps, had seen the brothers in action and called their hand. He turned loose six drovers on them, but Albert and Hobe pulled iron and drove the cowboys back into the saloon as they fired off their cannons and left Dalhart in a cloud of dust.

What these boys did not know, was that Dalhart, Texas was home to one of the best-known peace officers to ever wear a badge: Coyote Joe Colson. He earned this nickname from his uncanny ability to track fugitives. It did not matter if they were riding a horse or on foot, Joe had the instincts of a coyote when it came to hunting down outlaws. He was a master scout for the cavalry in his younger days and hunted down renegade Indians. Later, he pinned on a tin star and served as a lawman for the next three decades. The Letts would soon realize they had shot up the wrong town and garnered the attention of the wrong man—one of Texas' legends.

It just so happened that Coyote Joe rode into town minutes after the Letts had riddled the saloon with gunfire. The acrid smell of burnt gun powder still lingered in the air, and the sound of men walking over broken glass was all too familiar to this seasoned lawman. Amazingly, no one was killed or injured during the two-man shootout, which seemed quite strange to Colson. He could tell that the men who had fired the pistols had not intended to kill anyone. If they had, he would be looking at corpses rather than a bunch of cowboys staggering around inside the saloon. Still, someone had to pay for the damages and return the money taken from the drunk drover.

Coyote Joe gathered some additional information from some of the bystanders, including physical descriptions of the Letts, and promptly requested a fresh mount and a six-man posse. However, gathering a half-dozen able-bodied men from this bunch proved difficult, given that most, if not all of the men standing on the boardwalk, were three sheets to the wind. Colson pointed to six and told them to get their horses. But when the men attempted to mount, he knew immediately that in their present shape, they would endanger not only their own lives, but his. Coyote Joe wasn't about to ride with a band of fools. He waved his hand in the air and said, "We'll ride at first light if any of you drunk sons of Cain are able."

The next morning, in front of the livery, Joe climbed aboard his long-legged strawberry roan and peered up the street. There was not a single person stirring in Dalhart. He knew then, as he did the night before, that there would be no posse. He was accustomed to traveling alone anyway. After all, a volunteer posse of hungover cowboys was not Joe's idea of a winning hand.

Colson rode out of town and quickly cut sign of the Letts. Being a seasoned and wily tracker and lawman, he noticed from the hoofprints that one of their horses uncharacteristically threw out his right front hoof on the run. This would make it easy for Joe to stay on their trail if the brothers stayed on those horses. From the tracks and direction Albert and Hobe were headed, Coyote Joe believed they were striking for Lubbock, Texas. That was his gut feeling, and he was rarely wrong.

As a native Texan, Colson knew the lay of the land well, from every side trail to every draw and shortcut, and he did not hesitate to use them in hopes of getting ahead of his prey. Three days of hard riding, and the lawman reached Lubbock in the shank of the evening. He stopped in on Hank Sterling, the sheriff of Lubbock, who was an old friend. Joe described Albert and Hobe to Hank, and it was apparent the Lett brothers had not yet arrived. Sterling, like most sheriffs, kept his ear to the ground concerning his town, especially when it came to strangers coming through.

"Let's make a loop, Joe." He grabbed his hat and pulled it on. "We'll make sure these boys aren't amongst us." The pair of law dogs walked the streets of Lubbock, searching all four of the saloons in town. Then they walked up and down the boardwalks, from one end of town to the other, but the sheriff knew everyone they encountered. "Don't reckon 'em fellers you're after are here, pard."

"They don't appear to be, Hank. I've either got the steer by the horns or the tail. Right now, I'm not sure which." Joe wondered if he was ahead of the boys, or if they had turned away from Lubbock and gone in a different direction. Time would tell.

Colson and Sterling ate supper together at the diner. There they reminisced about the good old days as young lawmen. Each had been in his share of gunfights and manhunts. After supper, they made one more round through the saloons and down the boardwalks. Still, there was no sign of the pair. Joe was ready to turn in for the night. He and his horse had covered a lot of ground in the last few days. "Good night, Hank." He checked into the hotel up the street from the jail. As he lay in bed, he questioned himself as to why he was so far from home, looking for a couple of nibblers. Sure, they had left a lot of lead and holes in the saloon doors and fleeced a drunken cowboy, but they were not exactly what Joe would call dangerous highwaymen—not by a long chalk. Was it pride that had him in Lubbock, or his sense of duty to the badge? He wasn't sure, but he didn't tarry long trying to figure it out. His eyes were heavy from fatigue, and he soon fell asleep. He slept like a rock until the rooster crowed at daybreak.

When Colson awoke, he debated about riding north to see if he could pick up any fresh sign. He worried he might be in the wrong place, waiting for men who may never show. Sterling talked him into breakfast and encouraged him to stick around Lubbock for a few more hours. It was around noon when Joe decided to ride. He led his horse out of the livery and tightened the cinch. He tossed the stable boy two bits and swung up into his saddle. "Keep your powder dry, Joe," said Sheriff Sterling.

Joe tipped his hat to Hank. "You bet, friend, and you do the same. Obliged for the vittles this morning."

"Any time, Joe. Any time." Sterling threw a hand in the air.

Colson gigged his roan and trotted toward the north end of town. In less than a mile outside of town, he ran into two men he suspected might be the men he was hunting. As they passed each other, he nodded, as did they. Neither Albert nor Hobe could see Joe's badge beneath his coat, so there was no chance they knew him to be a lawman. And because Joe was headed north, toward Dalhart, the Letts suspected him even less.

Now, how could Colson be sure these were the Dalhart bandits? Being a quick thinker, Joe pulled his gun and fired in the air just a few yards from where he passed them. The Letts' horses spooked and took off running. Albert and Hobe finally got them settled down and turned back in the direction of the stranger. Each brother had his hand hovered over his pistol.

"What's that fool up to?" asked Albert.

"Looks like he's shootin' up in the tree," answered Hobe.

Joe was now thirty yards from them, staring up into a cottonwood with his pistol pointed upward. He wanted the boys to believe he was shooting at a squirrel or some other varmint. His plan worked, because Albert and Hobe turned their mounts toward the town of Lubbock and continued

41

without a second thought. When they got out of sight, however, Colson rode their way and dismounted where their horses had spooked. He wanted to see if either of their horses had thrown out a right front hoof on the run. Sure enough, one of them had. Joe now knew these were the men who had broken the law in Dalhart.

Coyote Joe made a wide loop and rode back into Lubbock, but this time he came in along a side road from the east. He tied off his horse at the blacksmith's hitching post and slowly crossed the street to the mercantile. From there, he spotted their horses—a chestnut and a sorrel—tethered at the water trough outside the livery. He noticed the men had removed their saddlebags and rifles, giving off the appearance that they planned to stay a spell. Joe was glad, for he was in no hurry to climb back into the saddle, so he sat down on the bench outside the diner and waited. He wasn't sure exactly where the men were, but knowing they were in Lubbock brought him a feeling of satisfaction. Just a few hours before, Joe had wondered if he was on a wild goose chase.

Sheriff Sterling walked out of his office and up the boardwalk. Joe saw him coming and pulled down his hat over his face, not wanting Sterling to recognize him. He feared his friend would give him unwanted attention, thus giving away his lawman status. But to his surprise, Hank whispered to him as he passed, "'Em fellows must have made it to town. I'll be across the street if you need me."

An hour went by before Joe saw any sign of the brothers. They came out of the bathhouse, wearing a fresh change of clothes and wet, slicked-back hair. They both kicked their boots together to knock off the dust, then they rubbed them against the back of their jeans. They pulled on their hats and looked up and down the street, each giving a final adjustment to their clothes and hats.

"Hobe, I'm hungry as a bear. Let's go yonder to that diner and get some vittles. How much money do you have on you, little brother?"

Reaching into his vest, Hobe pulled out three Lincoln skins. "Looks like we are down to the nubbins. That Dalhart's poke didn't get us far. We best visit the saloons tonight and go to work."

"Yep," said Albert with a chuckle. "The Lord helps those who help themselves. After supper, let's get the lay of the land and see who the big hogs are."

"I reckon it's wise to see how much law they have in Lubbock, too," said Hobe. Albert nodded, and they walked toward the diner.

Joe pushed up the brim of his hat and studied the boys. As a lawman, he could tell a lot about a man by how he moved—how he walked, his gestures, and such. He was sure that these fellows had no fear of being caught. Just before reaching the diner, however, one of them did something strange. He took a seat outside. Was he going to keep watch while the other ate? Had he seen something that spooked him? Or was he just being careful so the folks of Lubbock wouldn't know they were together? These questions and others were running through Colson's head.

Fifteen minutes passed before Hobe, who was sitting on the bench outside the restaurant, stood and went inside. He sat close to the back door, and Albert sat hunkered down in the back corner. These brothers had been on the lam long enough to know you never turn your back to anyone.

The waiter walked over and asked Hobe what he would have. Before Hobe could answer, both of them heard knocking on the door. "Excuse me, sir," the tall, slender man wearing an apron said, concern on his face. He pulled up on the latch and swung open the door. Standing on the threshold were two small boys wearing dirty, threadbare clothes. Both of them had smut on their faces. That, Hobe would learn later, was from cleaning out the ashes from fireplaces of the townsfolk to earn little, if any money.

"Boys," the waiter said with a hand cupped to his mouth as he looked over his shoulder and back to them, "I told you to come by after closing time. There should be some scraps today, and I'll make sure you get them. Now get, before Mr. Brewster has my hide."

Hobe could tell the waiter was a kind sort of fellow. He was in his early twenties and seemed to have a soft spot in his heart toward the hungry chaps. He even saw the tall lanky fellow wink at the boys as he shut the door. Returning to Hobe's table, he said, "I'm sorry, sir. My name is Henry. What can I get for you, the antelope stew or the buffalo brisket?"

"Glad to meet you, Henry. My name's Hobe. Reckon I'll have the stew. By the way," Hobe threw his thumb toward the door, "who were those young fellers beggin' vittles?"

"Johnny and Albert? They're orphan brothers who've had a hard time here in Lubbock. They—"

Suddenly, Henry was interrupted by someone loudly clearing his throat. It was Louis Brewster, the proprietor of the restaurant. "Taylor," he said gruffly, "I've told you about feeding 'em street rats. If I see you giving them food again, you're done here. You understand? Preacher or no preacher,

I'll not tolerate it. They can dig through the garbage for what we throw out, like the others."

"Yes, sir, Mr. Brewster, I understand." Henry nervously lowered his head and hurried to the kitchen to fetch Hobe's stew.

"Enjoy your food, son," said the big-bellied Brewster as he turned and walked away.

Hobe looked across the room at Albert and shook his head in disgust. He was livid that Brewster had spoken to Henry that way and that he had called the hungry boys street rats. But why did he refer to Henry as "preacher"? Hobe aimed to find out.

Henry bounded from the kitchen doors with a big plate of stew and some buttermilk biscuits. He placed them down in front of Hobe and said, "If you need anything else, just let me know." Henry began to walk toward another table.

"Well, there is one thing."

"Yes?" said Henry.

"Why did the big man call you 'preacher'?"

"Oh," chuckled Henry, "because I'm the pastor of the small church at the end of town. I work here to make a few extra dollars for my family. Mr. Brewster's been good enough to give me a job here in his restaurant. He's a churchgoer himself."

"Member of your church, is he?"

Henry chuckled. "No, not mine—the church off Main Street."

"I see," said Hobe. "Well, thank you, Pastor Taylor, for the stew and the excellent service. I reckon I'll see you at church Sunday. I'm a churchgoer myself. Might even bring my brother. You don't have any short benches, do you?"

"Short benches?" asked Henry with a slight, confused grin.

Hobe waved his hand and smiled. "Just pullin' your leg. I'll see you Sunday."

Hobe's words caused Henry's face to light up with excitement. "Well, Hobe, we'd be glad to have you. In fact, why don't you and your brother plan to eat lunch with us in our home? My wife, Sarah, is a good cook, and my daughter, Emily, well—she loves company.

"By the way," Henry said as a parting word, "don't come looking for no polished sermons. I'm just started, and, well, I've got a long way to go." They both smiled but were quickly interrupted.

Brewster, peering angrily at Henry, yelled from the other side of the room as he pointed at two men sitting at a table. "Get over here and take their order!" They were seated next to Albert, and this Lett, just like the other one, did not like the way Brewster treated the young man. Hobe and Albert looked at one another with equal displeasure.

Albert finished up his meal. He too, had eaten the antelope stew. He walked out the door and decided to take a quick tour of Lubbock. Given saloons were where the boys made their bread and butter, Albert walked by and surveyed all four of them, feeling confident that he and Hobe could soon put some jingle in their pockets. However, Albert was not traveling alone.

Coyote Joe saw Albert come out of the diner and followed him, but he did so in a manner that Albert never knew he was being watched. Hobe finished up his supper and went looking for his brother. He didn't know it at the time, but he too was under surveillance. Sheriff Sterling had assigned his deputy the task of keeping an eye on Hobe.

Albert saw Hobe before his brother saw him. But that's not all Albert saw. Sterling's deputy obviously had not learned the art of being discreet when trailing a man. He got too close, and Albert spotted him. On top of that, the deputy did nothing to disguise his badge. It was in open sight, shining like a new penny in the moonlight for all to see, and see it Albert did.

Colson noticed Albert's abrupt change in behavior when he saw the deputy. But instead of arresting Albert now, he wanted to see what these boys had planned for Lubbock. He waited for Albert to look the other way, and he waved off the deputy from following Hobe. Shortly after that, Albert put his fingers between his lips and whistled. In an instant, the Lett brothers disappeared.

In their hotel room, Albert explained his suspicions. "I don't know why that law dog was sniffing at your heels, Hobe, but he dang sure was."

"I swear, I didn't even see him. Reckon why he'd be following me?"

"Don't know," replied Albert as he peeked through the curtain and scanned the street from the hotel window.

"Maybe the law here in Lubbock is skittish about strangers. We best lie low until nightfall. Figure the Lucky Star Saloon is where I can do some good." Albert's idea of doing good meant that he was going to fleece the saloon's customers, especially those who were full of the spirits.

"You mean to go in there alone, Albert?"

"Yeah. You just stay put tonight. For some reason, the law has taken an interest in you, and I wouldn't want to have to explain to Ma how her Hobe got put in jail." Albert always believed Selah doted on Hobe, which she did. Even Julie, their sister, would agree. Hobe rolled his eyes and shook his head.

Albert waited until ten o'clock to leave the room and make his way to the saloon. He shimmied down a ladder on the side of the hotel that was used for a fire escape and scooted through the back alleys until he reached the Lucky Star. From the dark alley, he poked his head around the corner to the stoop. When he determined no lawmen were in sight, he stepped through the saloon doors and immediately scored on a drunken patron. They collided, as one man was coming and the other going. This was part of Albert's scheme, of course. He quickly apologized. "Excuse me, friend, for my clumsiness."

The drunk patted him on the shoulder aggressively and said, "No harm done, young feller." Obviously, he was unaware that Albert had picked his pockets, lifting his timepiece, coins, and nine dollars in paper money, without anyone seeing a thing. The Letts were not only fast with their guns, but they were greased lightning as well when it came to pickpocketing. No one was better than Albert.

Meanwhile, Hank and Joe sat outside the stoop of the jail eyeing the hotel, the only one in town, hoping at least one of the brothers would show. Two hours of sitting, however, had not netted them anything but numb behinds. "Let's make rounds," said the sheriff. "My tailbone's done took root in this chair."

Joe leaned forward and got to his feet. "I'm with you, pard. This is like waitin' for wet paint to dry. I've never been good at waiting. I should have nabbed that boy earlier today." Frustrated, Joe pulled off his hat and rubbed the back of his neck.

"Don't fret, Joe. We'll get 'em, yet."

The two lawmen visited three of the four saloons, but had no luck spotting the Letts. That is, until they bumped into Albert leaving the fourth as they were going in. He had his head down, so they didn't recognize him until he turned sideways, and Joe saw his profile.

Joe moved to the door quickly and walked out. Hank followed. "Seems that feller yonder who just walked out looks familiar," said Joe. They hurried into the alley, where Albert had walked, but he was gone.

They did not spot him, but Albert surely saw them, their badges and their six-shooters shining in the moonlight. He hightailed it through the back alleys and climbed back up the fire ladder leading to his room. As he stepped in through the window, Hobe said, "How'd you do?"

Albert emptied his pockets on the bed, and Hobe quickly counted the spoils. With excitement in his voice, he said, "There's perty nigh ten dollars here!" Albert didn't respond. He had something more troublesome on his mind: the law.

"Hobe, I figure our time in Lubbock will be short. There's law dogs sniffing around everywhere. I ran into two of them coming out of the saloon. Something tells me they're after us." Hobe looked curiously toward his brother.

"What I can't figure is, how'd they get word of what we did in Dalhart? That town didn't even have a telegraph office."

"I'm as buffaloed as you are, Albert. How could they be onto us? We've only been here a few hours."

"Well, dang if I know." Albert quickly changed topics as he plopped down on the bed. "Hey, what were you going on about in the restaurant earlier? You seemed to have it out for the big feller, the one who owns the diner."

"Yeah, if we're here long enough, I'd like to teach Mr. Brewster some manners, especially toward that young preacher-boy and those 'street rats' as he called them."

"Preacher-boy? You mean Henry?"

"Yeah, he pastors that little church we passed coming in this afternoon. A couple of young boys came to the back door for some grub. You ought to have seen them, Albert. Little fellows had black soot all over their faces." Hobe patted both sides of his face. "I figure they're cleaning chimneys or carrying out the ashes from the blacksmith's forge. They looked half-starved to death."

"Did Henry give them something to eat?"

"Well," Hobe hesitated, "he wanted to, but seems he was afraid Brewster would have his hide, and he almost did. He lit into him like a windmill in a twister. Told 'im if he feeds those boys again, he's done workin' for him."

Albert shook his head and started to answer, but Hobe interrupted. "Oh, Albert," he chuckled, "you'll get a kick out of this."

"What's that?"

Hobe grinned. "One of 'em street boys is named Albert."

Albert cocked back his head, pleasantly surprised, and smiled. "Well, I tell you, brother, a boy with the name of Albert deserves to be fed. Wouldn't you say?"

"That's what I was thinking. I recollect Henry calling the other feller Johnny."

"In the morning, how about you buying those fellers some breakfast at Brewster's? That will put food in their stomachs and give you a little entertainment as you watch the big man squirm. He ain't going to like them coming into his nice, clean establishment."

Hobe smiled. "No, he isn't. But you know what the Good Book says: 'When I was hungry you fed me.' That's straight from the Bible, Albert."

"Yes, it is, little brother. Figure to pay Parson Henry a visit and ask him where you can find the boys? I reckon he'd know. But Hobe, you be careful. Got me a twinge on the back of my neck about this town and them fellers wearing badges."

The next day, Hobe was at Henry's house early, knocking on the door. He expected the pastor to answer, but instead it was Sarah, and from the look of things, she was expecting a child in the coming weeks.

"Ma'am," Hobe said as he quickly removed his hat and held it between his hands, "I was looking for the reverend. Is he about the place?"

Before Sarah could answer, a little girl squeezed in between her mother's legs and gave the stranger a big smile. "You must be Emily," said Hobe.

Sarah looked surprised. "You know my daughter?"

"Yes, ma'am. I mean, I know of her. Pastor Taylor invited my brother and me to Sunday lunch and he—"

Before Hobe could finish explaining, Sarah said, "You must be Hobe. Henry told me he met a very nice young man at the diner named Hobe. He said you might be coming to church Sunday."

"Yes, ma'am, I plan on it. That is," he reached down and tickled Emily, who was coiled around her mother's leg, "if Emily approves."

Sarah chuckled and patted Emily on the head. "How about that, Emily? Would you like for Mr. Hobe and his brother to visit with us Sunday?" Emily gave a three-by-nine grin of approval.

"Mrs. Sarah, you can call me Hobe. I ain't old enough for the mister, yet."

"All right, Hobe." She continued with tears in her eyes. "You will never know how much you encouraged Henry by saying you would be coming to church. He came home happier than I've seen him in a long time, and I thank you for that."

Hobe was quickly transported back in time by Sarah's words. He remembered the struggles of his own father as a pastor. Often, he was upbeat when the church was well attended and discouraged when it was not. The look on Sarah's face was not unfamiliar either. Hobe had seen the same expression on his mother's face, as she often worried about her husband.

"We'll be prayed up and ready to hear what the Lord has to say through Pastor Henry. Mrs. Sarah, I was wondering where I might find those boys who came to the back door of the restaurant for vittles. I'd like to take 'em to breakfast at Brewster's Diner, 'cept, I don't know where to find them."

Sarah now understood what Henry saw in Hobe. Few times had she seen someone Hobe's age give a hoot about anybody but himself. She smiled and pointed up the street. "You can find Johnny and Albert hauling ashes from the blacksmith's shop and the houses of Lubbock—them and five of their friends."

"Ma'am, you mean there's five more boys as poor as Johnny and Albert?"

Sarah frowned and lowered her head. "Yes. Henry works two jobs, besides being the minister of the church, so we can help feed the seven boys who live in the alleys."

Hobe said incredulously, "You mean, Henry, excuse me, ma'am, I meant Parson Henry, works another job besides the diner?"

"Yes, he works for the blacksmith. He barters his labor for the use of Mr. Ludlow's lean-to. That's where the boys sleep at night."

"What about the other Christians in Lubbock? There's another church on the corner of Main Street. Looks like a right smart-size church. Does that parson and his congregation help the street boys?"

"Well, at one time they did. But…"

"What happened, Mrs. Sarah, if you don't mind answering my forward question?"

"Well," she said reticently, "one of the boys stole a coat. It belonged to a church member's child. Caused quite a stink. The church leaders told the parson they didn't want the boys to come anymore."

"Over a coat!" Hobe exclaimed passionately. Thoughts raced through Hobe's mind, taking him back to the painful times when the church leaders came to his house and demanded Albert sit the short bench and Julie, because she was expecting a child after being raped, be sent away. His face reddened, and he stared down at the front porch, trying to make sense of things.

Sarah could tell her words had disturbed him. "Hobe," she reached and put her hand on his shoulder, "are you all right? I hope what I said didn't upset you."

"Ma'am? Ma'am?" Hobe said as if he had snapped out of a stupor. "No, no ma'am. I was just thinking about the ugly side of religion, that's all. Seems like the Christians in these parts have forgotten Jesus' words about feeding the hungry and clothing the poor."

Sarah nodded in agreement but felt uncomfortable saying more. "Well, if you need to talk with Henry, you can find him at the diner around ten o'clock. That's when he starts his shift at Mr. Brewster's. If you need him earlier, he's at the blacksmith's shop up yonder." She gestured up the road.

"Much obliged, Mrs. Sarah. And I'll see you Sunday, Emily." He reached down and tickled the little strawberry blonde. She squealed and laughed through her missing baby teeth. Hobe acted as if he was leaving, but then he turned and tickled her again. Hobe and Emily were already becoming friends.

"Thank you, Mrs. Sarah, for the information. Got me an idea I'm going to chew on about them boys." He tipped his hat and left, whistling the tune, "Jesus Loves the Little Children."

Jim Burnett

A Banquet to Plan

When Hobe left the parson's house, he had a gnat in his hat, a notion that he hoped his brother would approve of. He walked into the hotel room, and immediately Albert suspected something. "Why are you acting the giddy goat?"

"Well, big brother, let me ask you something. You believe in the golden rule, right?"

Albert nodded. "Yes, I do. Do unto others as you would have them do unto you."

"Exactly."

"What you gettin' at, Hobe, or am I going to have to wait until Christmas to find out?"

"Albert, found me out something today about Parson Henry."

"Let me guess. He's an outlaw on the run. Murdered at least ten people and plans to do in a few more."

"Nah, ya bucket head."

"Then what, Hobe? What'd you find out about the parson?"

Hobe plopped down on the bed and grinned. "He's got a little girl named Emily and is expecting another child. His wife, Sarah, will be giving birth soon."

"Well, how about that. That's right nice," said Albert.

"That's not all. Found out more about those 'street rats' as Brewster calls them—them little fellers looking for grub. That's not all. Mrs. Sarah told me something right interestin' about Henry as well."

"Yeah? What's that?"

"Albert, that man works two other jobs besides being the minister of the church."

"What? You're pullin' my leg."

"Nope, and that's not all. His job with the blacksmith provides seven boys with a place to sleep."

"Seven? I thought there were two."

"Me too, until Mrs. Sarah told me different." Hobe stared in silence at his brother.

"All right, Hobe, what's up your sleeve? You planning some devilment? If so, I want in on it."

Both brothers laughed.

"Albert, I want to put on the feedbag for the seven at Brewster's. Also, I want to buy each one of them a new coat."

"Well, Hobe, that sounds swell, but where's the money for the vittles and coats coming from? All we've mustered since being in town is twenty dollars."

"Albert, we're in a town that's got many saloons. Let's get to work and fleece these sheep. Also, I want to visit that big church around the corner. Hear it has short benches."

"Short benches?" asked Albert, shaking his head and balling up his fist.

"Yep. Heard the good Christian folks who go there won't let the street boys come back to their church 'cause one of them stole a coat. Sounds like the good, religious folks of Pa's church."

"So," said Albert, "we have some of those kind of churchgoers in Lubbock, huh?"

Later that night, Albert and Hobe paid a visit to the church on Main Street, gaining access through an unlatched window. Sure enough, they found four of the wooden disciplinary benches on the front row. Both brothers' passions ran high as they yanked them off the wooden floor and hurled them out the back door and onto the steps. Then they hauled the benches outside of town on a borrowed cart and set them on fire. The sight of the burning benches brought both boys great delight. In some small way, they felt they were saving others from future humiliation brought on by those who practiced graceless religion—the kind they themselves had experienced.

For the next few nights, The Missionaries were on a mission: steal enough money from drunks to pay for the banquet for the seven street boys and give them each a new coat. Hobe even talked to Henry about it. He smiled at the idea but wondered how it could be funded.

After three nights of pickpocketing and rolling drunks in the alley, Albert and Hobe had lifted twenty-five dollars from their victims, plus they still had five of the twenty dollars Albert had taken a few nights prior. They were getting closer to the amount needed to treat the street boys to a fine meal and warm coats.

On Sunday, when the Letts went to Taylor's church, Pastor Henry floated the idea to his congregants. Although there were only twelve people there, the benevolent consideration went over well with those in attendance. Afterwards, Hobe and Albert went to the parson's home for lunch. Sarah cooked a fine meal, and the Letts enjoyed the food almost as much as spending time with Henry, Sarah, and of course, Emily. The time they spent around the Taylors' table, visiting and enjoying the delicious meal, brought back some fond memories of how their family had done the same so many times.

"Parson Henry," said Albert.

"Please, call me Henry."

"Obliged, Henry. What do you think about our idea?"

"Feeding the street boys and giving them new coats?" Albert nodded. So did Hobe. "I think it's wonderful. Don't you, Sarah?"

"I sure do, Henry. I sure do." She patted his hand with hers. Albert and Hobe glanced at one another and grinned. This man and woman had a deep love for one another. It was obvious. That gave the Letts a warm feeling.

"Me too!" shouted Emily as she climbed down from her chair and ran to Hobe, crawling into his lap. "We ought to feed them boys and give them coats. It's cold outside." Everyone laughed.

Sarah gently reprimanded Emily. "Emily, shouldn't you ask to sit in Hobe's lap before plopping down?"

"Well, shucks, Ma, I figured he liked me as much as I like him." That brought more laughter and a quick response from Hobe.

"I sure do like you, Emily, and you can sit on my lap any time you want."

"Fact is," said Albert, "Hobe and I have a niece just about Emily's age. Her name is Danielle, after our pa, Dan. Seeing Emily puts me in mind of her, and I figure it does Hobe, as well."

Hobe nodded. "Yep, and Danielle's about as silly as Emily." Hobe tickled Emily. She squealed like a pig, squirming and stretching in response.

"Now, back to this banquet and coats," said Henry. "We'll need a right smart of money."

Hobe moved Emily to his knee, playing like he was giving her a horse ride, moving her up and down. He stopped and looked around her toward Henry. "Albert and I have thirty dollars to throw in the pot."

"Thirty dollars!" exclaimed Sarah. "That's mighty kind of you both to give that kind of money, but won't you need that for your travels?"

"Oh, no, ma'am," said Albert. "The Lord always takes care of us. Besides, we can fetch more where that came from." Albert glanced at Hobe and smiled.

"Well," said Henry with a somber face, "I spoke with Mr. Brewster about the idea when you first mentioned it. He didn't warm to it. Fact is, he said no. Said at no price would he allow the boys to eat his food in his establishment.

Thought I could talk him into it, but, well…" Henry shrugged his shoulders and raised his hands. "I'll just leave it at that."

"Pastor Henry," said Hobe, "sounds to me like Brewster's wantin' to feed the boys for free. Didn't he say at no price would he allow the boys to eat in his place?"

"Yeah," chuckled Henry, "but I don't reckon he meant it that way."

"Poor ol' Mr. Brewster," said Albert. "I figure he's got enough money to burn a wet elephant." Again, everyone laughed. Sarah waved at Albert with a wrinkled face and soft rebuke.

Henry continued with optimism. "I did speak to Mr. Spikes, at the mercantile. He was a little more receptive than Mr. Brewster about helping, especially when I told him we wanted to buy seven coats. The way I figure, we will need thirty-six dollars for the coats. That's not including food."

"Well," said Hobe, "if I have my figures right, we're only shy six dollars."

"Less than that, Hobe." Henry counted out three dollars onto the table.

"Parson, I mean, Henry," said Albert, "you and Mrs. Sarah should keep that for yourselves, with the little one coming and all."

"Yeah, and you might have to buy Emily some teeth with that money." She was missing a couple. Again, Hobe poked Emily in the side, and she giggled.

With tears in his eyes, Henry said, "Albert, you and your brother have been generous enough to come into a town full of strangers and want to feed and clothe some hungry street boys. That means a lot to Sarah and me."

"Me too, Pa," Emily spoke up as she quickly climbed down out of Hobe's lap and left the room.

Henry's face puckered, and he shrugged his shoulders at Sarah and the Letts. "That Emily. You never know what's going through her pretty little head." As he spoke these words, there were loud noises coming from Emily's room. Sarah excused herself to check on her.

When the two of them returned, Sarah was crying, and Emily wore a smile a country mile wide. She placed her two nickels on the table and said, "Now we should have enough."

It was a tender moment. Nobody could speak for a few seconds. Henry scooped his daughter up in his arms and said, "Emily, you remind me of the woman in the Bible who gave her two coins. You know what Jesus said about her?"

"No, Daddy, what?"

"He said she had given more than all the others that day because she gave all she had."

Hobe wiped the tears from his eyes, as did Albert. This exchange between Henry and Emily brought back many memories of Dan sitting down with his boys and talking to them about the things of God.

Henry wiped his eyes with his sleeve and said, "Well, we still need a couple of more dollars for the coats and food."

"I'm believing that Brewster's goin' to feed them boys out of his own pocket. That's what I'm believing," said Hobe.

"Me too," said Albert. "Pastor Henry, when should we have the feed and give the boys their coats?"

"Figure it will take two weeks for the coats to arrive. Sarah and I can get the boys' measurements. All 'cept Butter are about the same size."

"Butter?" said Hobe.

Sarah frowned at Henry, and with a slight grin, she said, "His name is Otis. He's a short fellow, and he's a little broad in the beam."

Henry held up his hands and said jokingly, "Very broad in the beam."

"Henry," rebuked Sarah, "that's not very kind." They all laughed, knowing that Henry was kidding.

"So, when should we plan this shindig for the boys, Pastor Henry?"

"Well, Albert, if we get the coats ordered tomorrow, I figure two weeks from Monday." Henry rubbed the back of his neck. "But I can't figure Mr. Brewster changing his mind."

"Why don't you let me jaw with him," said Hobe. "I've eaten in his diner a few times since being in town. Maybe he'll be a little more willing with a paying customer."

Henry shrugged his shoulders and nodded his head. "Maybe so." Sarah smiled and patted Henry's hand.

Two days later, Hobe was having lunch at Mr. Brewster's diner, and he took the opportunity to float his idea by the owner. "Mr. Brewster, there's a few of us here in town who would like to have a banquet of sorts here in your fine restaurant."

"A banquet, you say? What's the occasion, Mr. Lett?" Brewster asked as he moved his cigar from the right side of his mouth to the left and sat down in the chair across from Hobe. The thought of making a few extra bucks excited the entrepreneur.

"Pastor Henry and a few of us would like to bring in the boys who live on the streets for a good feed. Want to make the night really special for them. Those fellers have had a hard time trying to make a go of it, especially this winter."

Brewster frowned, and his cigar dropped from his mouth onto the table. He grabbed it up and brushed away the ashes. "Them guttersnipes, in my restaurant? Not as long as I'm breathing."

"Well, now, Mr. Brewster, I heard you were a churchgoing man, a Christian."

"I am a Christian!" insisted Brewster as he slammed his fist on the table. "But business is business, and I ain't about to allow that scum in my place." He pointed toward the street. "I'd lose customers. Besides that, they'd steal me blind. No, sir. I won't allow it."

"Well, Mr. Brewster," Hobe said as he stood up and grabbed his hat from the table, "I figure you stand to lose more than customers if you rain on these boys' parade."

"What do you mean by that, Lett?" Brewster's posture toward Hobe changed, along with how he addressed him.

"I hope you won't have to find out, sir. It's a bad thing turning away hungry folk. Jesus said if we did that, he'd deny that He ever knew us." Hobe continued to speak to Brewster as if the owner had capitulated. "Now, what we're planning for the chaps shouldn't take up much room. That big table over yonder in the corner will do." Hobe pointed, but Brewster refused to look. He balled up his fists and grunted.

"You deaf or somethin'? I told you, I'm not interested. Now, I'm sure there's another place in town where they—"

"No, sir." Hobe reached down and tapped the table. "This is where we'd like to have it. You've got the nicest place in town, and those boys deserve a little taste of Heaven for a change."

Brewster, red-faced and madder than a bear with a sore tooth, leaned into Hobe. "Mr. Lett, I've tried to be cordial with you, but if you can't respect my answer, then I'll just say goodbye and good day."

Hobe tipped his hat and grinned. "And a good day to you, Mr. Brewster." In his mind he was thinking, *It's probably the last good day you will have for a while.*

The seven coats for the boys were ordered, and Hobe insisted that they continue planning the banquet meal at Brewster's, even though the owner was vehemently opposed. Mr. Brewster had even lit into Henry, during his next shift, for thinking his establishment was a good choice for the celebration. Nonetheless, Hobe insisted that the meal would take place at Brewster's. Albert agreed with his brother.

The next day, Hobe arrived at the diner for breakfast, but there were no customers in the restaurant. A sign that read *CLOSED* hung on the door. Hobe tapped on the door, and through the glass he saw Mr. Brewster coming toward him. He flung open the door and said abruptly, "We're closed."

"Well, Mr. Brewster, if you don't mind me asking, why are you closed? I sure am hungry for some of your catheads and redeye gravy."

Gruffly, Brewster responded. "Three buckets of lard spilled in the kitchen. It'll take the rest of the day to get it cleaned up. Closed until then." Brewster started to close the door.

"Well, I declare," said Hobe. "Anything I can do to help?"

"Obliged, but no," answered Brewster. "Now, if you'll pardon me, I've got to get back to work." He quickly closed the door.

The next morning, the restaurant reopened, but as bad luck would have it, the kindling used for firing the stoves was wet and wouldn't burn, no matter how hard the cook attempted to get it lit. Apparently, the pump leaked overnight, and water seeped out onto the wood that was stacked beside it. Customers lined up at the door, ready to eat breakfast, but Brewster reluctantly turned them away. "Sorry for the inconvenience, folks." He threw his hands in the air. "Had a leak in the pump. Kindling is wet, so we can't light the stoves. Come back for lunch. We'll have plenty of food ready for you."

Hobe was one of those in the front of the line. When Brewster finished his announcement, the two of them locked eyes. "Sure hate all this bad luck coming your way. If there's anything I can do, let me know."

Brewster shook his head and mumbled, "What I need is some dry kindling." Under his breath he whispered, "But where would I find some?"

"Well, Mr. Brewster, let me see what I can do. I think I know where I can put my hands on some." Brewster didn't even respond, as if he didn't hear him. Just before the door closed, Hobe said, "I'll be back in three shakes of a lamb's tail. Mr. Brewster, did you hear me?"

"Yes, I heard you, Mr. Lett. I'd be much obliged. I'm sort of in a bind."

Thirty minutes later, Hobe walked through the back alley leading up to the restaurant and knocked on the back door. Brewster's cook, Roger, greeted him.

"We're closed, mister. If you could come back—"

"I'm Hobe Lett. Is Mr. Brewster here?" Hobe ducked his head inside the door and looked around for the owner. "Brought him some kindling for his stoves."

The cook was excited. "Well, come on in! We sure need some dry wood. I'll fetch Mr. Brewster."

Brewster came quickly, just in time to see three small boys, each carrying in an armload of kindling. "Where you want this, sir?" asked the chubby fellow everyone called Butter.

Brewster hesitated and then stuttered. He couldn't believe what he was seeing. Coming to the rescue of his restaurant were the same guttersnipes he had forbidden to allow in his place. "Uh, set it down over here, boys."

Hobe brought in an armload himself. "Mr. Brewster, maybe this will last you until yours can dry a spell. If you need more, me and these boys here know where to get it."

Brewster looked at Hobe with a little bit of suspicion and a whole lot of gratitude. "Thank you, Mr. Lett and... boys. This should get us through. How much do I owe you?"

Butter cleared his throat and started to speak until Hobe snapped his fingers. "Mr. Brewster, you don't owe us nary penny, sir. We figured it was just the Christian thing to do, didn't we, boys?"

The three chaps looked at Hobe curiously, and after reading his gesture, they quickly turned to Mr. Brewster and said, "Yes, sir. The Christian thing to do." They really didn't have a clue as to what Hobe was talking about, but they went along with their new friend, hoping somehow it would be advantageous to them. At the moment, they didn't know how right they were.

As the boys walked out the door and into the alley, Hobe tipped his hat to Brewster. "Good day, sir." He stepped toward the door.

"Mr. Lett," said Brewster as he extended his hand. "Much obliged for your help."

Hobe reciprocated and said, "Glad we could help, sir. You know the Good Book says to do unto others as you would have them do unto you. I figured if I were in your shoes, I'd like someone to bring me some dry wood."

Hobe sensed Brewster beginning to soften, but he wasn't quite there yet. Perhaps one more crisis would put him in a generous frame of mind.

Two days later, another problem cropped up in Brewster's kitchen, about an hour before the breakfast crowd. The stovepipe wouldn't draw. The kitchen filled with smoke and wafted into the dining area. "What now?" yelled the furious Brewster to his cook as he rushed into the kitchen with his hands in the air.

"The blame pipe is blocked with creosote, I reckon. We need a chimney sweep." Roger, the cook, worked for a while to unclog the pipe, to no avail. Brewster, with a look of disgust on his face, hung the closed sign on the door again as people walked toward the diner. Hobe was the third person in line for breakfast.

"Sorry, folks," said Brewster with a frown. "Stove pipe is clogged. Come back around lunch and we should be open."

As Brewster began to close the door, once again, he saw Hobe staring at him. He was now beginning to wonder if his harsh stance toward the street boys was the root of his problems. Maybe the Lord was chastising him, or was it Lett creating all these problems? Brewster didn't know for sure, but it certainly got him to thinking.

About fifteen minutes after Brewster closed his front door, there was a knock at the back door. It was Hobe and two more of the street boys, different ones than had brought him dry wood the day before.

"Mr. Brewster, I heard you might be in need of a chimney sweep. These two boys, Albert and Johnny, clean lots of chimneys in town and would be glad to clean your stovepipe."

Again, Brewster hesitated. "Uh—yes, uh, come on in, fellas. Stove's over there." He pointed over to where Roger was fretfully and uselessly shoving a broom handle up the pipe in hopes of clearing it.

Albert walked over with his tools and said, "If it's creosote in them pipes, mister, it ain't coming loose poking at it with that broom handle. Me and Johnny will get up yonder on the roof. Have her cleaned out lickety-split."

Within minutes, the pipes were echoing and vibrating. The two little chimney sweeps were at their trade, making the pipes sing. Albert was using a long metal rod to dislodge the soot. Oddly, however, when they finished, there in the kitchen, in the bottom of the stove, there was little creosote to show for their cleaning. Nevertheless, the pipes were clear, and the stove began drawing again when the cook lit a fire.

Brewster turned to Hobe and said, "Mr. Lett, you and those boys have once again saved my bacon."

Albert and Johnny came back into the kitchen. Their hands and faces were black with the stove smut. But this time, Brewster treated them differently. "Here, boys." He handed them a towel. "Come over to the pump and wash your hands." He pumped the handle while they held their dirty hands under the water.

The boys were shocked at Brewster's kindness. The last words they had heard from him before had been, "Get out of here, you little varmints, or I'll crease your head with this stick."

When the boys finished washing up, Brewster asked, "How much do I owe you, boys?" He pulled out a wad of money from his pocket.

"No charge, Mr. Brewster. Figure we owe you for some of the food Henry has given us over the last few weeks. And seeing that it's the Christian thing to do, me and Johnny are glad to help."

The boys went toward the door. Hobe followed them.

"Mr. Lett," said Brewster.

"Yes, sir," answered Hobe as he shooed the boys out the door.

"It would be my pleasure to serve up a meal to these young fellers and their friends, on the house, of course. What day did you say was best?"

Hobe grinned and shook Mr. Brewster's hand. "How about next Monday? Could we plan to have supper for them?"

"Next Monday is fine. Just let me know what they like to eat, and I'll have plenty of it."

"Much obliged, sir. Good day to you."

"And to you, Mr. Lett."

Hobe left the diner with a three-by-nine grin. His plan to bring Brewster to the table, or at least get him to allow the guttersnipes at his, had worked. Hobe had shown Brewster what Christianity looked like at the hands of the street boys, even though his method of doing so was less than pure. Between Hobe and Albert, they had masterminded the lard spill, the wet wood, and the blocked stove. No one needed to know that except the two brothers, and maybe Albert and Johnny, the chimney sweeps. There was just no way of getting around telling them that a coat had been stuffed in the top of the pipe.

Hobe and Albert were anxious to tell the Taylors the good news. That evening, they dropped by for a visit. Henry and Sarah were amazed at how Mr. Brewster had changed his mind toward allowing the street boys to have supper at his restaurant.

"The Lord surely works in mysterious ways," said Henry.

"Yes, he does," said a smiling Sarah.

Henry looked at Albert and Hobe with a smirk. "Seems that ever since we spoke with him about having the boys to his diner, he's had lots of problems—spilled lard, wet kindling from a leaking pump, and a blocked stovepipe."

Hobe smiled. "Yes, sir. I think Mr. Brewster was like the young Belshazzar of the Bible. He saw the handwriting on the wall."

Sarah and Henry, again, marveled at these boys' knowledge of Scripture. They hadn't been in Lubbock long, but the Taylors were growing closer and closer to these two. However, Henry wasn't quite as gullible as some might think.

That night, as the Letts left, Henry stepped out on the porch to say his goodbyes and a little more. "Albert, Hobe, I'm obliged down to my boots that you two are helping our town orphans."

"We're glad to help, Parson," responded Albert. Hobe nodded in agreement as they went down the steps.

"Fifty-pound lard cans don't get spilled by themselves. The leaking pump and wet firewood—well, maybe. And Roger told me that when Albert and Johnny finished cleaning the pipe, there wasn't no more than a handful of creosote. That wasn't enough to keep that stove from drawing."

Albert and Hobe held their poker faces. "Well, Pastor," said Albert with a very slight grin, "I'm thinking along the same fence line as you. But as Mrs. Sarah said, 'The Lord does work in mysterious ways.'"

Hobe waved at Henry. "Have a good night, Pastor Henry. And give Emily a hug for me."

***

Coyote Joe and the sheriff of Lubbock had not given up their hunt for the Lett brothers. In fact, they had patterned the boys' movements. They knew now that Albert and Hobe were fleecing saloon customers up and down Main Street. It was just a matter of time before they would make the arrests.

What seemed strange to the lawmen was these boys' connection to the parson and his family. They had seen Hobe and Albert in and out of Pastor Henry's home several times. Why would a preacher allow the likes of these thieves in his home?

One Saturday night, Hobe and Albert were seen on the boardwalks of Lubbock. Coyote Joe was called to the scene, and he and the sheriff determined they were going to collar the boys this night. The brothers walked into the Boar's Head Saloon and went straight to the bar to begin their work for the night. Joe eased through the doors, sat at a corner table, and watched them, inconspicuously, for over an hour. Never had he seen partners work together so adeptly. They were smooth as silk and fast as lightning. Still, at worst, they were nibblers, pickpockets. But then Coyote Joe remembered how they had shot up the Dalhart saloon, and he was resolved that they would at least be held to account for the cost of the doors. After all, Coyote Joe's reputation was at stake.

The sheriff and his deputy sat outside, waiting for a signal from Joe. The Texas lawman pushed through the doors and sat down next to them. "Yep, it's them. 'Em boys are cleaning those old cowboys' plows. I'm going to bring the youngest one to you. Stay right here."

Joe eased back into the saloon and went straight to the bar. He positioned himself next to Hobe, slowly drew his pistol, and put it to his belly. "Son, that's a .44 Colt aimed at your gut. Hand me your shootin' iron, but slowly. Don't make no quick moves. You both are covered."

Hobe did as he was told. "Now, walk toward the door and don't look back." Again, Hobe did as he was told. Sheriff Sterling and his deputy jumped to their feet as Hobe came out. "Over here, young man," said Hank. "Have a seat. I imagine your brother will be joining us directly."

"What's this about, Sheriff?" Hobe asked as he saw the reflection of Hank's badge in the coal lamps next to the saloon doors.

"Let's get your brother in harness, and I reckon we'll have us a good jaw."

A couple of minutes later, Albert walked out on the boardwalk, followed closely by Joe. "All right, boys," said Hank, "you've beat the Devil around the stump long enough. Goin' to put you up in the jail tonight. Hear you got some damages to pay in Dalhart. Joe will be jawing with you on that score."

The next morning, Coyote Joe worked the key back and forth in the lock and opened their cell. "Come on out, fellers. I watched you boys fleece them whiskey guzzlers last night. Frankly, I figure a man who has no better sense than to get drunk gets what he deserves. But I'm holding you boys accountable for shootin' up Mule Townsend's saloon. Figure you owe him for a couple of new doors. Figure twenty dollars should cover it."

Albert stuffed his hand in his pocket and pulled out some money. He had twelve dollars. He looked at his brother. "Hobe?"

Hobe quickly grabbed at his pockets. He came up with the balance and put it in Albert's hand. "Here's the twenty, Mr. Joe."

"You boys best find a new line of work. I don't abide thieves. But like I said, a fool who gets liquored up deserves a fleecing. Then again, I got a mind to pack you fellers back to Dalhart."

"Well, Mr. Joe, we'd be obliged if you didn't. We're puttin' on a feed for seven street boys tonight. Givin' them coats to boot. Right up yonder at Brewster's Diner. Most of the money to pay for that came from what we've taken from the saloons. Know it ain't right, but we couldn't abide these boys going without."

The three of them walked out on the jail stoop. Joe stepped down and untied his roan. He stuffed his boot in the stirrup and climbed aboard. Reaching into his vest pocket, he pulled out a ten-dollar gold piece and flipped it to Hobe. "Put that toward helping them boys." Joe wheeled his horse and rode for Dalhart.

That night, seven boys were treated like kings as they feasted on roast beef, fried potatoes, gravy, and biscuits, followed up by all the apple pie they could eat. Even Butter got his fill, which rarely happened. When the meal was over, Pastor Henry's church members brought in the new coats. The smiles shining from the seven boys' faces would never be forgotten by anyone present, not even Mr. Brewster. It was worth all the effort that had gone into pulling off the banquet, even though it almost got the Lett brothers extradited to Dalhart. But thanks to the good-hearted Coyote Joe, he cut them some slack. Although he didn't tell them at the time, he too had been an orphan, raised on the streets and back alleys of Laredo, Texas. If it weren't for a generous old couple taking him in, no telling where Joe would have ended up.

Jim Burnett

A Mother's Plea

Selah Lett would hear from her sons from time to time. They had come to Garden City twice since taking up their guns for evil. Albert and Hobe enjoyed the visits with their mother, their sister, Julie, and their little niece, Danielle. But they never stayed long. Julie had married a young man who was serving as a deputy to the sheriff, so the brothers kept their distance, out of respect for him and their sister. Up until now, their crimes had not garnered the attention of many lawmen and bounty hunters. However, that was about to change.

Unfortunately, in Eagle Springs, Kansas, during their last bank robbery, Albert shot one of the tellers who pulled a gun on Hobe. The brothers got away with over five thousand dollars in cash, but sadly, the bank teller died from his wound. Consequently, a reward of ten thousand dollars was placed on each of the Letts' heads. Selah knew that her sons were now living on borrowed time. They would be hunted and killed if found in the sights of the right person. So, she prayed and spoke with her father-in-law, a retired minister. He suggested they contact Lucas and Levi Reese, of Caldwell, Kansas, two legends of the frontier known for wearing their badges and toting their guns under the authority of God. These twin brothers were now federal lawmen—Lucas, a marshal, and Levi, a deputy marshal.

Pastor Lett wrote a letter to his good friend, Jarvis Doran, a minister in Caldwell who happened to be Lucas Reese's father-in-law. This man had a heart for prodigals and responded empathetically. He agreed to speak to Lucas on behalf of Selah, but also encouraged her to personally write Lucas about her sons, which she did.

Dear Marshal Reese,

My name is Selah Lett. My sons, Albert and Hobe Lett, are on the run from the law. Last week, as I am sure you have heard by now, a man was killed during a bank robbery in Eagle Springs. My sons were the ones who robbed the bank. Now there is a reward of twenty thousand dollars out for them.

Marshal Reese, I know they must be held accountable for their actions and punished. But as their mother, I can't abide the thought of someone shooting them down like dogs. I am writing for your help.

I have heard from my father-in-law, as well as many others, how you and your brother, with the help of God, brought law and order to Caldwell, and how you have been very successful bringing in those outside the law.

My husband, Dan Lett, was a pastor before he died a few years ago. It seems my boys believed his death was the fault of church people. We did have some painful experiences at the hands of religious folks, but that is no excuse for the devilment of my sons.

I know that I am asking a lot, but if you and your brother could find and bring in my sons, I would be much obliged. Though they have taken the wrong road, they are still my sons, and I love them dearly.

Sincerely,

Selah Lett

Lucas read the letter from Selah and shared it with his brother, Levi. Both men felt a strong desire to take up the hunt for the Lett brothers. One reason was the fact that when the Letts robbed the bank of Eagle Springs, they had crossed into the Reeses' jurisdiction. But the second and bigger reason they took up the hunt was because of Selah's letter. Within that letter they heard a mother's plea for mercy on her sons.

Jim Burnett

Brothers Hunting Brothers

Jarvis Doran met and prayed over Lucas and Levi Reese the next morning, before the two lit out of Caldwell in search of Albert and Hobe Lett. Just as they got outside of town, Lucas had a feeling someone was following them.

"Got me a little twinge on the back of my neck."

Immediately, Levi knew what his brother suspected. "Lucas, when we get around that bend up yonder, I'll peel off and wait for our company. Probably those two bounty hunters who've been sniffing around. They were real interested in the Letts' wanted poster tacked to the board out front."

Lucas nodded, and as planned, when they reached the bend in the road, he kept going, leading the packhorse. Levi tied off in the brush and waited.

Sure enough, two men came riding by. The bounty hunters Levi had seen in Caldwell the previous day were following them. "Stand easy, boys," said Levi as he stepped from the brush with pointed gun. "Now, fellers, it ain't healthy to ride another man's tracks, especially if he don't want you to. Where you headed?"

"Ain't no law against riding down this here road, is it, law dog?" One man stepped down from his bay and lowered his hand over his pistol.

His actions brought a swift reply from Levi. "Mister, I can see you been brought up on sour milk, and you ain't real smart. But if you get back on your horse and ride the other way, you can go on breathing."

Lucas held a bead on the second rider from a knot forty yards away. He knew his brother was fast enough to take both men, but he was in no mood to take chances. The Lett brothers needed to be found, and found quickly. Right now, they were burning daylight.

Levi lowered his hand over his pistol, and said, "Your call, mister."

The other fellow, riding the palomino, seemed to be a little smarter than his friend. "Let's go, Jess. We've got business elsewhere." Perhaps he wondered where Lucas was and why the brothers had split up. Or maybe Levi's confidence shook him. Whatever the reason, he gave no thought to bracing Levi and showed much eagerness to leave.

The man standing on the ground frowned. "I don't cotton to being told where I can go. I like the direction we're headed." He waved his hand in the air.

Levi read the man's mind and pulled iron. Just as he did, the fellow reached for his. Feeling merciful, the deputy marshal strategically placed his bullet into the right shoulder of his challenger, sending him to the ground. Then he quickly turned his gun to the other man, asking him if he wanted some.

"Not me, mister. We're just trying to make a few dollars. You know them Lett brothers have a right smart bounty on their heads."

"Yeah, but I catch you following me and my brother again, you'll never look at another wanted poster."

Levi, still with drawn pistol, stepped into the brush and led his horse to the road. He climbed into his saddle and gathered his reins. "You need help gettin' 'im on his horse?"

"Obliged, but I can manage." The man seemed to be in a hurry for Levi to leave.

Lucas, still holding his rifle on the man in the saddle, shook his head. He knew that when the other feller had braced his brother, he was about to die, or at best, leave with serious wounds. He was right.

Levi tipped his horse in Lucas' direction and gave him a nudge. Within minutes, he caught up with his brother. "You sure ain't making no time, brother."

"Well, I didn't know if that feller ridin' the yeller was game or not. Anyway, I needed to stretch my legs, having ridden so far and all." Actually, they were less than half a mile out of town.

Levi chuckled. "Okay, Lucas, let's get a wiggle on."

The brothers rode hard for the next week, making their way toward Eagle Springs, checking in with lawmen as to the whereabouts of the Letts as they traveled through different towns.

After their last robbery and the killing of the bank teller, the Letts were lying low. They had plenty of money, but their high-profile status kept them from showing their faces, especially during the day. Like other highwaymen, they would have to rely on less than honorable men to buy their supplies and keep them hidden, hoping not to be sold out.

The heavy reward placed on their heads brought bounty hunters from all parts of the country, like bees to honey. But it also brought another brand of men to the hunt: the dreaded Pinkertons.

The Pinkerton National Detective Agency was a private security guard and detective agency, founded in 1850 by a man by the name of Allan Pinkerton. The Pinkertons were a tenacious bunch, often hired by banks and railroads to protect their gold and cash. Since Albert and Hobe cottoned to robbing both, they had gained the attention of this agency.

The Pinkertons worked with local law enforcement across Kansas to cast a wide net in hopes of catching the Letts. But the brothers were careful not to show themselves. They did their moving around at night.

As Lucas and Levi got closer to Eagle Springs, they were seeing more and more bounty hunters. The lawmen they knew said there were more of them than you could shake a stick at. The large bounty on the Lett brothers turned a lot of farmers, store owners, and jobless men into man hunters. Lucas and Levi had seen this before—trigger-happy, money-grubbing men, and even boys, in a feeze. The thought of pocketing the twenty thousand dollars in bounty on the Letts created fierce competition and deadly consequences.

Lucas and Levi were out on the plains, scouting for sign, when they rode right into the middle of a gunfight. Elbert Green and his two sons, Jake and Brownie, were hunkered down in a drain, defending themselves in what looked like an attempted ambush. Three hundred yards away, the Reeses saw smoke from the barrels of two rifles. Lucas grabbed his field glasses, trying to figure out the situation. He looked to his right and saw the father and sons, their guns blazing, and to his left, two men returning fire.

At first glance, it looked as if the man and his sons were under attack and were pinned down. But as the lawmen sat their horses, lead whizzed over their heads. The shot did not come from who the Reeses suspected were bounty hunters; it came from the other direction.

"Let's get to cover!" said Lucas. They rode into some tall grass and dismounted, with rifles in hand. "Ain't sure which end is which, Levi," said Lucas. "Reckon why that feller shot at us?"

"I don't know," said Levi. "Maybe he thinks we're with that other bunch. I figure the only way to get to the end of this is to go down yonder where that last shot came from." Lucas nodded in agreement. "Want me to circle around behind these other fellers and bring 'em to the table?" asked Levi.

"Yeah, but watch your top knot. These plains are full of hostiles. Ain't sure who these shooters are, and if that's all of them."

It took each of the lawmen about twenty minutes to snake into position, being careful not to get shot in the process. Levi reached the bounty hunters first, or at least that's who he thought they were. "Deputy Marshal Reese, boys. Shuck 'em rifles and put up your hands."

To Levi's surprise, the men didn't say a word as they put down their weapons. They looked to be hill people, ridge runners, some called them. "Why are you shootin' at that man and his boys?"

"Deputy," the tall skinny man said as he slowly turned toward Levi, "we was riding along, scouting for antelope sign, when that fool down yonder and his boys commenced to flinging lead at us. We got to cover and been defending ourselves."

Levi, having been a lawman for three decades, knew men. He had a knack for deciphering someone telling the truth or not. He believed the man's story. "You fellers aren't bounty hunters, hunting the Lett brothers?"

"Naw, Deputy. We's hill people, trying to get us some meat," answered the tall man. "Nathan Bidwell's my name." His partner nodded but didn't say anything. Levi could tell something wasn't right about the little fellow. Then Nathan made some hand motions to his partner. Levi realized he was a mute. "Who's the Lett brothers?" asked Bidwell curiously as he looked back at Levi.

Levi was certain now that these men were on the level. "You can pick up your rifles. My brother should have them others in hand by now. Reckon we'll head down yonder and get things straightened out." Levi gestured with his head. Then a shot rang out. Then another. And another.

"You men get your horses and be on your way. Your story sounds plumb to me. Appears the problem's over there where my brother is." Levi hurried to his horse and ran to the gunfire. When he got closer, he saw Lucas pinned down by the three shooters. Levi whistled and got Lucas' attention. He gave his brother the signal that he was going to make a wide loop and flank the three.

Lucas raised up out of the tall grass and fired two quick shots at the men who had been shooting at him. "I told you fellows that I'm a United States marshal. Throw down your guns, or somebody's going to get killed."

The older man among the boys yelled, "We know you're after the Letts, and we aim to claim the bounty on them. So, get on your horse and ride away, or me and my boys will kill you for sure." Another flurry of shots rang out, and lead whizzed over Lucas' head.

Levi got into position where he could see the three men lying in a drain about fifty yards out, an easy shot with his Winchester. He had them in his sights, all of them, but hoped they would drop their guns and stop acting like fools. Levi raised up on a knee and aimed at the older man's lower back. "Deputy marshal! You men are under arrest!" he yelled. "Throw down your guns and throw up your hands."

Unfortunately, the old man wouldn't give up so easily. He must have thought Levi was Lucas and there was only one of them. "Kill that law dog, boys. Kill 'im dead."

All three of them turned their guns on Levi. That proved to be a deadly mistake. Rifles fired and smoke wafted across the plains. When the shooting was over, Elbert, Jake, and Brownie Green were fatally wounded. When Lucas and Levi got to the drain, they came from different directions.

Brownie, the oldest of the two boys, had just enough breath in him to tell the brothers his name, along with his pa's and younger brother's. He was scared to die and cried out in pain, "Don't let me die. Don't let me die!" Lucas held Brownie's head off the ground with his hand. Then the boy's body began to quiver, and his eyes flung open. It was a ghastly sight.

Levi shook his head in disbelief. "Pa always said the love of money is the root of all evil. Reckon Mr. Green had a bad case of it. Even poisoned his sons with his greedy ways. It's a darn shame."

Lucas was visibly shaken. He knew his bullet had cut down at least one of the boys, maybe even both. "What a waste." Angrily, he waved his hand over the three and said, "This didn't have to happen. Let's get 'em buried. Don't want the coyotes eatin' on 'em."

The Reese brothers were seasoned lawmen, and they had killed their share of men, but never a father and two young sons. They dug the graves and stacked the rocks over them without saying a word to each other. When finished, they each removed their hats and lowered their heads. "These are days that make me want to give up the badge," said Lucas.

"Yep, I know what you mean, brother."

That evening, they camped about a mile away from where they had buried the Greens. They unpacked their gear and built a fire. Neither said much. The wood crackled as the flames turned it into coals. Levi put a couple more sticks on the fire and reached for the coffee pot. "Man at the pot," said Lucas with a smile. Levi poured him a cup and said, "Reckon where those Lett brothers are? That bounty on their heads is making folks crazy."

"I've been figuring on that myself, brother—the whereabouts of those boys and just what got them in this spot. According to their ma's letter and Pastor Jarvis, they aren't killers."

"Yeah, well, tell that to the bank clerk who was gunned down."

"Well," said Lucas, "I know they killed that man, but that fool shouldn't never snatched iron."

"Lucas, am I hearing you right? You saying it was the clerk's fault for getting himself killed, and not the Letts'?"

"Nah, but," Lucas removed his hat and scratched his head, "there's something about Mrs. Lett's words that tells me these boys are not all bad. Yeah, they done wrong and need to be brought to heel. I just hope they'll fare better than the Greens."

"Amen to that, Lucas. Don't ever want to have to kill another boy. They were just kids."

"Yeah, but their Winchesters didn't know that. Their guns were spitting lead just like their pa's."

"Yep, you're right about that. But," Levi shook his head, "dying between hay and grass, that just ain't right."

Three days later, Lucas and Levi Reese apprehended Hobe Lett. They found him in an abandoned cave, on a hunch from a lawman they had come across. Hobe was so distraught from seeing Albert killed that he could hardly think straight. It had been two weeks since his brother's death, and Hobe had been hiding out ever since. He was so skinny from not eating that he could have bathed in a gun barrel.

Lucas and Levi stepped into the cave and identified themselves as they called out Hobe's name. He gave up his guns without a fight. A sadder looking fellow they had never seen. He wouldn't even make eye contact with them. The Reese brothers were transporting Hobe to Caldwell, Kansas, but on the way there, the marshal and deputy marshal had to use their guns and badges to convince bounty hunters to give them the road or die. There was no way the Reeses were going to let anybody take Hobe from them.

Amazing Grace

Hobe sat on the bunk in his cell in Caldwell, staring down at the floor. For hours, he did not move, except to gesture his rejection of food and water, as well as any conversation Lucas and Levi offered him. Likewise, he waived his right to the defense lawyer provided to him. Albert's death shook Hobe down to his boots. He and his brother believed they were on a mission from God, as bizarre as that sounded. But when Albert killed the clerk in Eagle Springs, the brothers, for the first time, questioned their actions. They had never before killed, and they regretted it terribly.

Many thoughts were racing through Hobe's mind. He was angry that his brother was shot by a bounty hunter and sad that he was dead. Hobe was also afraid of hanging.

Lucas sent Selah a telegram, communicating to her that Hobe was in custody in Caldwell, Kansas. He also informed her that Albert was dead. Three days later, Selah, along with Reverend Elvin Lett, Hobe's grandfather, arrived to visit him.

"Hobe," said Lucas, "you've got a visitor. Your ma is here."

Lucas' words drew a quick response from Hobe. "I don't want her to see me like this. Please, Marshal." Hobe grabbed the steel bars. "Don't bring her in this cell."

"She's come a fer piece to see you, son. It was your ma who asked my brother and me to fetch you boys. She didn't want you two shot down. We were too late to help Albert, but son, you got to live."

Hobe frowned and lowered his head. "I don't want her to see me in this cell."

"I'll tell her, Hobe, but, that's your ma out there, son."

Lucas opened and closed the door that separated the cells from the larger room where Selah and Reverend Lett were waiting anxiously. Hobe stood in the corner of his cell with his head down. More than ever before, he wanted to see his mother. He wanted to hear her voice and feel her hug. But he genuinely wanted to spare his ma and his elderly grandfather from seeing him jailed.

With his ear against the wall, he heard his mother sobbing, which caused him great sorrow. Tears rolled down his face as he whispered, "Ma, I'm sorry, Ma." Hobe stepped back and leaned against the wall and sobbed. The thought of hurting his mother, the one who loved him more than anyone in the whole world, was unbearable. But then he heard his cell door unlock. He was so distraught that he hadn't noticed Lucas come through the door and unlock his cell.

"Come on out of there, Hobe, and see your ma and grandpa."

Hobe quickly wiped his tears and stepped forward. "Much obliged, Marshal."

"Mr. Lett," Lucas said as he pulled on the cell door, "ain't puttin' hand irons on you. Want to spare your mother the sorrow, but you will be covered." Lucas patted his pistol. "Don't do nothing foolish. Go out yonder and comfort your ma."

"Yes, sir," responded Hobe. "Ain't going to give you no trouble."

When Hobe walked out, his mother ran to her son with open arms. He fell into her arms and wept. Lucas and Levi both lowered their heads and looked away out of respect. It was a very emotional time for everyone in the room.

"Ma," Hobe gently pushed Selah away and looked her in the eyes, "Albert's... dead."

"I know, Hobe. I know."

He buried his head into her chest and sobbed.

Albert and Hobe Lett's devilment had come to an end—a deadly one for Albert. Selah and Hobe's grandfather spent about an hour with Hobe this day, telling him about Julie and her family, and all that was going on in Garden City. Before they left, Selah pleaded with her son to speak with the town's defense attorney.

Over the next few weeks, the Reese brothers and Pastor Jarvis Doran spent a lot of time with Hobe, talking, playing checkers, and even praying with him when he'd allow it. Never had Jarvis Doran seen anyone so balled up and confused about religion, other than himself years ago, right after the death of his wife, when he took to the bottle.

Pastor Doran took a liking to the young Hobe. They had many conversations about the Bible, about God, the church, Hobe's father, and church people. Little by little, Hobe began to open up to the old parson, and what was deep in his heart was worse than ten gallons of strychnine.

Hobe's resentment over his father's premature death and the cruel treatment of church people toward his family seemed to be the catalyst for his and his brother's criminal ways. Jarvis empathized, for he knew the hurt he felt when his wife died years ago. He prayed and prayed that God would heal her, but she died anyway. That led him to become a drunk and abandon his family, that is, until the Lord got a hold of him through the efforts of his son-in-law, Lucas Reese.

"Son," said Jarvis to Hobe, his hand on his shoulder, "you've been through the mill, and your soul is bruised. You've taken out your anger and hurt on folks everywhere you've been. Oh, you and your brother, from what I've been told, did a lot of good for people. But Hobe, until you face up to your wrongdoing, God can't heal your heart, my boy."

Hobe respected Jarvis. Whether that was because he was a pastor or because he had shown him such love and kindness was unclear. Maybe it was both, but the truth spoken from Pastor Doran this day pricked Hobe's heart. He jumped up from his bunk. "My pa loved those church people, and they killed him!" Hobe beat against the wall with his fist. "It ain't right, Pastor Doran, that church people— Christians—would act that way." For the next few minutes, Hobe went on a rant until he collapsed back onto his bunk, breathless, sullen, and sad.

"They made my brother sit on the short bench for a whole month, but the fellow who drove the carriage was forgiven, just 'cause his pa had money." Jarvis was not sure what Hobe was talking about, but he listened intently anyway. "Made my little sister, Julie, who got raped by a stranger down by the creek, leave town, like she was a criminal. They were ashamed of her being with child when it wasn't her fault." Hobe sobbed, and his face turned blood-red, but Jarvis knew the poison in this young man's soul was being expelled. Hobe continued.

"My ma, she's an angel. Wouldn't hurt a gnat. But so many times I saw her crying over what mean church folk said about my father. They also left her out of the women's socials. We acted like we didn't know because we knew that would make her even sadder. But we noticed. We knew. We saw her tears. And now, I'm the cause of her sorrow."

"Hobe, I lost my wife some time ago. I was so mad at God that I began to drink, get drunk, and stay drunk. I even walked out on my son and daughter, left them to fend for themselves. I was a preacher, but I had lost faith in God. Gave up my church and gave up on life."

Hobe turned to Pastor Jarvis and gave him a curious look through tear-filled eyes. "What brought you back, if you don't mind me asking?" He wiped his nose with a handkerchief.

Jarvis was happy to answer. In fact, he took Hobe's question as a confirmation the Lord was working. "You know that marshal who brought you in? He's the fellow who saved my life and helped me back into the pulpit."

"You mean Marshal Reese?"

"Yes, sir. He married my daughter, Rachael. She once was a saloon girl when she first came to Caldwell."

"Mrs. Rachael, that sweet, pretty lady who's brought me my meals?"

"Yep, the same one. Tell you what," Jarvis said with a smile, "the next time she comes in, I want you to say, 'Mrs. Penny, tell me your story. And tell me about Jarvis Doran.'"

Hobe was now intent on listening as he sat down on his bunk and stared up at Jarvis. "Call her Mrs. Penny? Sure she won't light into me?"

Jarvis chuckled. "No, but she will tell you that God is a forgiving God. He'll heal your heart. You see, Hobe, you may think church people are your problem, but they aren't really. It's how we react to life that either makes it good or bad."

"You sound a lot like my pa, Parson Doran. He told my brother and me many times that the Devil is crouched at the door, tempting us to sin."

"Sounds like your father was a godly man who trained up his sons in the way they should go."

Hobe quickly finished the quote from Proverbs twenty-two: "So when he's older, he'll not depart."

"That's right, Hobe. That's right. You have hidden God's word in your heart, haven't you?"

"Yes, sir, I have. So I would not sin against Him."

"How about this verse?" Jarvis asked. "Do not merely be hearers of the word, but…"

"But doers," Hobe answered quickly.

"Well, son, I'd better go." Jarvis stood up and pulled his big black Bible from the table.

"That's a mighty big Bible you have there, Pastor Doran."

"Yes, it is, with a mighty big message. How about you hold on to it for me for a couple of days? Read it and tell me your favorite passages at my next visit."

Hobe nodded, humbled by the pastor's offer. "Obliged. I'll take good care of it."

"I know you will, son. I know you will." Jarvis patted Hobe on the shoulder.

Lucas walked through the door just in time to open the cell. "You fellows about tired of looking at each other?" he asked with a smile.

"Marshal," answered the old pastor, "you better watch your step. Hobe's got my big black Bible, and he's going to be reading it. He catches you out of step with the Lord, he might remind you with some Scripture." Jarvis winked at Hobe as he stepped out of the cell and turned.

The moment the two men left, Hobe broke open Doran's big black book. He had not read the Bible in years. The pastor's notes littered the margins, and Hobe soaked up all of them. The marked-up Bible reminded Hobe of his father's Bible, which was given to Hobe shortly after Dan's death. For the first time since Hobe was a child, the words on the pages seemed sweet and consoling to him. It took him back to when he and his siblings sat at the feet of their father, next to the fireplace, and listened as he read the Bible to them. Being locked in a cell, awaiting his trial, made this young man think about a lot of things. Much about his past was painful, which seemed to be the reason that he and his brother had taken up their outlawing ways, but not all of his memories were bad.

Hobe remembered his father taking him and Albert fishing and giving each of them their first pocketknives. He remembered picnics down by the creek, and how they skipped rocks across the water. Dan could make his rock dance, often getting as many as four skips. Hobe smiled as he thought about this. Hobe's dad was also a wonderful storyteller. He would have Hobe and Albert in stitches as they listened to his experiences growing up. Those were good times, sitting on the creekbank without a care in the world. He remembered one day when Albert slipped and fell in the water. Instead of Dan scolding him, he stripped off his clothes, jumped to his feet, and went headfirst into the water. Hobe wasted no time in joining them.

When the three got home that afternoon, Selah wondered if they had taken leave of their senses. This made them laugh even harder as they stood on the porch dripping wet and scantily dressed. Selah did not see the humor. She was only thinking of the extra work of washing the clothes they had used to dry themselves. But her seriousness finally gave way to a smile. Julie fought the urge to laugh, out of respect for her ma, but when she saw Selah smile and say, "I ought to take a hickory switch to the lot of you," Julie cupped her mouth and chuckled.

As Hobe relived those experiences, his face lit up, and for the first time since being arrested, he grinned from ear to ear.

"Hobe—Hobe!" Rachael called as she stood there with his breakfast and coffee.

"Oh, hello, Mrs. Reese."

"Are you all right, Hobe?"

"Yes, ma'am, I am. Just thinking about some good times I had with my family when I was younger."

Rachael smiled. "My father, Pastor Jarvis, said you and he have become good friends."

"Yes, ma'am, reckon we have. He left his Bible for me to read." Hobe held up the black, leather-bound book and patted the cover.

"Well, you must be mighty special to him," responded Rachael. "I've never known my father to lend out his Bible to anyone. That's the one my ma gave him for an anniversary gift."

Hobe's eyes lit up. "Sure enough? Well, I am obliged for the use of it. Given what you said, makes this book even more special."

Rachael handed Hobe his tray of food through the bars. "Well, Hobe, you are special."

Hobe looked up at Rachael. "Thank you, ma'am." Then Hobe remembered what Jarvis had told him. He took a deep breath and grinned. "Mrs. Penny, tell me your story, and tell me about your father, Jarvis Doran, if you have the time, ma'am."

"That daddy of mine's been talking, has he?"

Hobe smiled and nodded. "Yes ma'am, reckon he has."

For the next twenty minutes, Rachael shared her past: the tragic death of her ma, and how her father, who was a minister, became a drunk. Tears rolled down her face as she described the experience of preparing her mother's body for burial. Sadness was in her voice as she spoke of her brother, now known as Cool Hand Luke, who had taken up the gun and was still on the run. Rachael explained how Lucas Reese, her husband, took a shine to her and her father, and what he did, with God's help and others', to restore her father to his right mind and ministry. She even talked about her salooning and separating men from their money.

Hobe hung on her every word. He couldn't take his eyes off Rachael, not just because she was beautiful, and she was, but because of what she was saying. Up until now, Hobe Lett felt he was the only one on Earth who'd ever experienced the depth of pain and disappointment he had endured. But sitting in a chair on the other side of the steel bars was a woman who had been through hell and back.

Rachael wiped her tears, and her facial expression changed. "Hobe, now let me tell you what Jesus did for me and my dad. My saloon name was Penny. One day, a big man, wearing a tin star, walked into the saloon up the road and saw my worth. He was the sheriff of Caldwell."

"Reckon you're talking about Marshal Reese?"

"That's right, Hobe. Lucas was the sheriff at the time. He was the first man who ever made me feel that I had worth. Wasn't long after we met that my father came to town, drunk. People laughed at him, and rightly so. For a shot of whiskey, he would tell you a rib-cracking story. He played the town clown wherever he went. Perhaps fool is the better word."

"Pastor Jarvis Doran?" asked Hobe skeptically.

Rachael nodded. "Yes, Hobe, Pastor Jarvis Doran. I was angry at my father for years. He left my brother and me to bury my mother. I'll never forget that day. After the funeral, he came home carrying a case of whiskey. He had already drunk a couple of bottles. When we needed him the most, he wasn't there. We were asked to leave the parsonage where we lived. Dad had become a drunk, and the church wouldn't tolerate a drunk pastor."

"Church people," Hobe said with disgust as he wagged his head.

"Well, Hobe, those church people were right. Some men tried to help my father. They wanted him to sober up and continue to lead the church. But he was so mad at God and in love with whiskey that he turned them down. My brother and I ended up leaving together, and that's when I started salooning to make a living. That's where I got the name Penny—from taking men's money."

"You, Mrs. Rachael? That's hard to figure, seeing how you are now and all."

"Yes, Hobe. God is a gracious God, a forgiving God, a restoring God. You see, I was raised in a minister's home, and I knew a lot about the Lord, but knowing about him and knowing him are two different things. The Lord gave me a new start."

"A new start. That sounds mighty good. But I'm afraid it's a little late for me. Looks like I have a rope that's got my name on it. I'll hang, for sure."

"Hobe, it's never too late with God. You don't strike me as the kind of man who would kill another."

"No, ma'am. I ain't never killed nobody. Never even aimed my gun at a feller in hopes of hitting him. It was my brother, Albert, who shot and killed that man in Eagle Springs. But he didn't want to. He told the fellow to drop his pistol. It was aimed right at me." Hobe lowered his head. "When we heard that man had died, it made us do some thinking. Taking another man's last breath will do something to a feller's innards. It sure did take a toll on Albert. I never saw him so sad. He wished over and over that he had never shot that feller. Several times at night I had to settle him down from a nightmare. He would yell and scream, 'Don't shoot 'im, don't shoot 'im!' It was awful."

Rachael knew firsthand what Hobe was saying to be true. Several times, when Lucas came home from hunting men he had to kill, she witnessed him acting oddly for several days, as if something was stuck in his craw and he had to work hard to get it choked down. Rachael tried to talk with him about the experience, but Lucas would clam up. He didn't want his wife to be troubled. It was not until she spoke with his brother, Levi, that she understood what her husband was going through. Levi's wife experienced the same thing with him. Killing just didn't sit well with a man of conscience. And although a lawman beddin' down an outlaw was part of the job, it was the part that the Reeses never got comfortable with. Lucas and Levi were both still dealing with the pain of having to kill the Greens when they were hunting the Letts.

"Hobe, did you tell your story to your lawyer?" asked Rachael.

"Parts of it."

"Did you tell him that Albert was the one who shot the man?"

"No, ma'am, I didn't. My brother's dead, and I don't want to run down his name."

104

"I understand that, Hobe, but you could hang if you don't tell all the facts."

"I'll think on it, Mrs. Rachael. The crazy thing about it is, neither Albert nor myself were able to spend the money we took from that bank. Shucks, after that killing, we couldn't go into a town except late at night. Men were huntin' us."

Rachel grabbed the bars of the cell, and her facial expression changed. "Hobe, are you saying that you never spent the five thousand dollars?"

Hobe chuckled. "Nah, it's tucked away in some saddlebags, buried outside of Eagle Springs."

Rachael stood up. "Would you be willing to give back the money?"

"I reckon so. Ain't going to be needing it where I'm headed."

"Could you find the money again if you went there?"

"Yes, ma'am. I know right where I put it, 'lessen somebody found it."

"Hobe, enjoy your breakfast. I'll be back to see you soon." Rachael picked up her purse and smiled as she pointed her finger. "And you keep reading that Bible, you hear?"

Hobe stood and tipped his head. "Yes, ma'am. Going to get back to it right after I eat these vittles."

Rachael had grown fond of Hobe, and found him, like her father and the Reeses did, to be a very kind and decent young man. Now, with the information she had, she felt certain that his life could be spared from a rope. She rushed to find Lucas to tell him the news. Perhaps if the judge heard that Hobe did not pull the trigger that killed the clerk, and that he was willing to return all the money, he would have mercy and not sentence Hobe to death.

Within an hour, Rachael returned to the jail, but this time she brought company—her father, Hobe's lawyer, and Marshal Reese. "Hi, Hobe. How was your breakfast?"

"Well, hello again, Mrs. Rachael. My breakfast was mighty tasty. Thank you, ma'am," Hobe said nervously as he saw the other men. "I didn't expect to see you again this soon."

"Hobe, I want you to tell Mr. Fonteyn what you told me earlier. He believes it may help your case before the judge."

Hobe, with puckered face, nodded and sat down on his bunk. For the next few minutes, Hobe shared, in detail, what happened at Eagle Springs—how Albert shot the clerk, and how they buried the money a few miles outside of town. He agreed to Mr. Fonteyn's request to go and dig up the money, with the provision that Marshal Reese and his brother, Levi, the deputy marshal, be the ones to take him there.

Joe Fonteyn, Hobe's lawyer, received written permission from the judge, who commissioned the Reeses to escort Hobe and retrieve the money. They left town under the cover of darkness late that night. But as wily bounty hunters often do, there were some hanging out in Caldwell with their ear to the ground. Somehow, word had leaked of the Reeses' plans.

As Lucas and Levi boarded the nine o'clock northbound train to Wichita, with Hobe chained between them, Lucas carefully eyed the two men who sat down behind them. He had no doubt they were bounty hunters looking to score the loot. Lucas leaned over to Levi and gave him the news. But given the three of them would have to travel the length of the entire state of Kansas to get to Eagle Springs, they felt they had plenty of time to shake those hunters loose.

To break the monotony of travel and to give the bounty hunters something to chew on, Lucas whispered to Hobe, in a voice loud enough for the nosy bounty hunters to hear, "Now, you sure you can locate that money, Mr. Lett?"

Levi picked up on his brother's ruse and quickly and conspicuously scribbled out a drawing on a piece of paper, labeling several places. Emporia, Kansas was one of them. It was the next town where the train was scheduled to stop. There were arrows on the paper pointing from Emporia to Osage City. Levi also included a rock formation, trees, and a creek. Beyond those, an arrow pointed to an x, which supposedly marked the spot where the money was buried. Levi slipped the paper to Hobe and told him to pretend it came from his pocket.

"Yes, sir, Marshal. I have the drawing right here." He held it up where, if the bounty hunters were looking (and they most certainly were) they could see it, which they did. Levi acted as if he had nodded off. When he woke up, he scolded Hobe for holding out the drawing where everyone could see. He grabbed the paper and wadded it up as if he was mad. Then, the deputy marshal eased out of his seat and looked around to see if anyone was showing interest in the drawing. The bounty hunters quickly looked away.

Levi sat back down and elbowed Hobe. The three men fought hard to supress their laughter. When they reached Emporia, the two men sitting behind them bolted for the exit.

Lucas shook his head. "Levi, you sure put a knot in their tails. They'll be in Osage City before daybreak." Again, the men laughed. Then Lucas turned to Hobe with a serious look and whispered, "You do know where the money is?"

"Yes, Marshal. But it ain't where that drawing said it was."

The men stepped off the train and wet their whistles at the nearest saloon. When they finished, they walked outside to the boardwalk just in time to watch the bounty hunters race down the street on horses they had rented from the livery.

"Well," said Levi, "reckon where they're headed in such a jo-fired hurry?"

"If I was a betting man," responded Lucas, "I would say them boys are strikin' for Osage City, huntin' that x on the paper." Grinning, Hobe shook his head.

It took a couple of days to reach a place called Atchison, Kansas. That's where Hobe and the Reeses left the train and unloaded the horses they had brought from Caldwell. It was a thirty-mile ride to Eagle Springs. Again, shortly into their trip, these lawmen, legends of the Kansas frontier, suspected they had company.

"Let's hole up in them cottonwoods yonder, Levi," said Lucas. "Rest these horses and get our bearings."

Levi thought it a little strange, stopping so soon, but he could read his brother like a book. "Got that twinge on the back of your neck, do you?"

"Yeah. We're being followed."

Hobe spoke up. "There's a dogleg off to the right up here, a narrow path Albert and I used many times to shake loose trackers. It's got a little bluff where you can see for miles. But we'll have to do it right to get them to take the bait."

"All right, Hobe," said Lucas. "Show us how it's done."

He gathered his reins and gigged his horse. "Follow me."

The three took off running down the road, then veered off to the left onto a stony path. They traveled that path for a quarter of a mile, and it brought them back around to where they started. Then they took the dogleg off to the right. They lost whoever was following them.

Lucas and Levi were beginning to see how Hobe and his brother had managed to elude the law for so long. They had grown wise in their outlaw ways. Before the Reese brothers returned to Caldwell with Hobe and the stolen money, they would see Hobe display more of his skills.

As they got closer to where Hobe had buried the money, they noticed a lot of men in the area. There had always been the rumor that the Letts had buried the money right outside of Eagle Springs, but somehow word had reached the area that the marshal was bringing back the surviving Lett brother to retrieve the money. This created a dangerous life-and-death situation. To disguise themselves, they removed Hobe's hand irons and their badges. As Levi glassed the area ahead, he saw six men riding hard toward them. Lucas checked his gun, as did Levi.

"I can stop 'em if you want me to," said Hobe.

"Son, we can't let you kill those men."

"Marshal, I ain't never shot a man and don't plan to today. Lend me your Winchester, and I'll split up that bunch and stop 'em in their tracks."

Levi again glassed the men. "That's a rough-looking lot coming our way. Ain't none of them wearing badges, either. Figure there's a range war in the making here, but not over grass, cows, or water." He peered at Hobe. "Reckon they want to put their brand on you, Mr. Lett."

"Hobe, how far are we from where the money is?" asked Lucas.

"About six miles, as the crow flies, I figure."

"Got anymore doglegs we can take to get out of sight?"

Hobe nodded. "Yes, sir, Marshal. Sure do. If we can get to that knot up yonder before they do, I can make us disappear."

"Take a miracle to get there before them, the way they're ridin' those horses," said Lucas as he rubbed his chin.

"No, sir, just a couple of well-placed shots."

Lucas looked at Levi, trying to read his thoughts. "What do you think? Should we let Hobe take a crack at 'em?"

"I reckon so, else we're going to have us a gunfight on our hands. There's six of them and three of us, two with guns."

"Well," said Lucas as he pulled his rifle from his scabbard and pushed it toward Hobe, "there's three now. Hobe, we're putting a pile of trust in you, boy. Take your shots, but remember what I said."

Hobe nodded and cranked down and up on the lever, sinking a cartridge in the chamber. He laid his hat on a rock that was nose level and placed the gun on top. Slowly and methodically, he looked down the steel sights and adjusted for windage. Leaning his cheek against the stock, he adjusted his position and gently squeezed the trigger. Levi watched through his field glasses. The lead from the rifle ricocheted off three different rocks. Hobe quickly racked another in the chamber and climbed aboard his horse. "Let's ride for the knot." The Reeses jumped into their saddles and spurred their horses.

Hobe's shot stopped the riders, but now they were again barreling their way. So, Hobe pulled up and waved Lucas and Levi around him. "Keep riding for the knot." Hobe threw up the rifle and cranked off another round. This time he shot off one man's hat. The group of six bailed off their horses and crawled to cover. By the time they got their rifles into shooting position, Hobe and the Reeses were out of sight.

The angry men emptied their rifles toward the high ground, even though there was no target in sight and no return fire. For the next fifteen minutes, a thick cloud of burnt gun powder settled over the shooters, hindering their vision and causing them to cuss and fidget. They peeked over the rocks they were behind and decided to slowly maneuver up the hill. When they reached the top, there was no sign of Hobe and his escorts. They had indeed, as Hobe said they would, disappeared.

But men don't just vanish into thin air. Where did they go?

There was a narrow tunnel at the top of the knot that Hobe and Albert had slithered through many times. It came out a quarter of a mile down the hill. Lucas and Levi led their horses behind Hobe's. Finally, they saw daylight. When they exited the tunnel, they were surrounded by a small stand of aspens, completely out of sight of those pursuing them. The lawmen and their prisoner mounted and gathered their reins.

"That was some fine shootin', Hobe," said Levi. "Probably saved us some blood and lead. And that tunnel—mighty slick back door you and your brother had."

Hobe grinned. But each of them knew there was no time to bask in their escape. "We best get out of here before them ol' boys cut our sign. Lead the way, Hobe," barked Lucas. "Let's get to where we're going."

Hobe spun around on his horse with his reins in his left hand and the Winchester in his right. "Here's your rifle, Marshal." He tossed it to Lucas. "I'm proud you trusted me."

Lucas tossed it back. "Hang on to that smoke stick. I figure before we get this money out of the ground, we may have to fight to stay out of it ourselves. You're too good a shot not to be gripping that rifle. But remember, don't shoot anybody unless you have to. Be hard enough explaining to the judge why you're toting iron and not wearing it."

Levi chuckled. "Yep. We might all end up in Leavenworth."

"Yeah," said Lucas, "it ain't but a whoop and a holler from here."

That evening, the three men made camp roughly five miles from where Hobe believed he'd buried the saddlebags stuffed with money. As they lay awake under a sky full of stars, Levi asked Hobe a question that set him to telling of his and his brother's exploits across the West.

"Coyote Joe—you ever heard of him?" asked Hobe. Before Lucas or Levi could answer, he continued. "Well, he's a lawman from Dalhart, Texas. He tracked Albert and me to Lubbock. Didn't even know he was in town 'til one night he slipped a Colt to my ribs and told me to walk outside."

"Why was Coyote Joe after you?" asked Levi as he refilled his coffee cup.

"Man at the pot," said Lucas as he held his empty cup toward Levi.

Levi shook his head. "Brother, you get me every time. Someday I'll have you filling my cup."

"Not likely. That'd be like catching a weasel asleep." Hobe grinned as he listened to the brothers banter back and forth. It made him miss Albert even more. "You may be faster getting that hogleg out of leather, but when it comes to the cup, well, I'm just a little quicker to the draw." Lucas winked at Hobe.

"Go ahead, Hobe," said Levi as he shook his head. "Tell us about Coyote Joe and why he set his cap fer you."

"In Dalhart, Albert and me fleeced a drunken drover. The bar dog, Tiller Townsend, demanded a cut of our takin's. We weren't in the mood to share. He set the rest of them cowboys on us. They had blood in their eyes and ropes in their hands. But Albert and I sent 'em back inside with their tails tucked. Sort of shot up Townsend's doors doing so."

"Coyote Joe followed you to Lubbock for shooting up a saloon door and fleecing a cowboy?" asked Levi incredulously.

"Yup. I couldn't believe it myself until I felt his cold pistol barrel poking my gut."

"Well, Hobe," said Lucas, "what did old Joe do next?"

"He arrested Albert and me and said we were going back to Dalhart to face up to what we'd done. But when we told Coyote Joe that we were planning a feed for the orphaned boys of Lubbock, he decided to check out our story with Pastor Henry, one of the parsons in town. We didn't know at the time, but after he put us in the cells he went and spoke with the preacher. After jawin' with him, the strangest thing happened."

"What did he do?" asked Levi.

"The next morning, Coyote Joe opened the cell and told us we owed twenty dollars for damages in Dalhart. After we paid him, he walked outside, stepped up on his horse and tossed up an eagle. 'That's to help pay for 'em boys' coats and vittles,' he said. Then he tipped his hat and rode out of town."

"He didn't know you boys were wanted?" asked Levi.

"No, sir, I reckon not. Had he known, I reckon our goose would have been cooked. Albert and I looked crossed-ways at each other as we watched Joe ride away."

"Tell me about the coats and vittles Joe mentioned."

Hobe nodded. "There were seven boys living on the streets of Lubbock when we got there. The church folk weren't doing much to help them, except for Pastor Henry and his small congregation. So, we got together and talked a stingy restaurant owner into letting us have a banquet for these fellers. You haven't never seen the likes of seven hungry boys eating until their bellies couldn't hold no more, and wearing their new coats to boot." Hobe slapped his leg and chuckled. "Albert and I sure did enjoy that night. I believe the pastor and his family did as well."

As he and the Reeses sat around the fire, Hobe went on to recount the many towns and cities he and Albert had visited, righting the wrongs they saw, especially with those who called themselves religious folks. Lucas and Levi were surprised at how these brothers finagled and got people to help. Albert and Hobe were indeed champions of the underdogs—those who had little and were doing without. In fact, the lion's share of the money they stole went to helping the less fortunate folks they came across. That still didn't make it right, and now Hobe would have to pay.

Nonetheless, Lucas and Levi were taking a shine to Hobe. This young man had done some wrong things and made some bad decisions, but from what these lawmen could see, Hobe Lett had a heart of gold.

The next day, the three of them rode, without incident, to where Hobe had buried the money. Levi stood on a ridge, cradling his Winchester and providing cover while Lucas stood next to Hobe with gun in hand to protect him from anyone who might try to take the money or their lives. Hobe pulled the shovel from behind his cantle and used it to pry up the rocks. He flipped over two of them, and there were the saddlebags. Lucas pulled open the flaps, and when he saw the money, he barked, "Let's ride!" He whistled to Levi, and the three of them left in a cloud of dust. Several days later, they returned to Caldwell with Hobe and the money.

When they rode into town, they noticed more people on the boardwalks than usual. Strangers were present—a lot of them.

When Lucas stepped into the jail ahead of Hobe and Levi, he was met by Rachael, holding a telegram from a Kansas judge. Somberly, she handed him the paper, which read, *Upon the return of the money, I'm granting a stay of execution for Hobe Lett. He is to be extradited to the Leavenworth State Prison in one week where he will spend the rest of his life.* This was good news, but to Lucas it didn't register that way. In his mind, he didn't believe Hobe Lett should receive such a harsh sentence. Rachael agreed.

"This isn't right," she said. "That boy shouldn't be going to Leavenworth."

As Hobe climbed down off his horse, he heard a familiar voice. It was Pastor Henry Taylor, of Lubbock, and his wife and daughter. "Hello, Hobe."

Hobe's face lit up, and his eyes widened. "Pastor Henry, Mrs. Sarah, and Emily!" He reached down to tickle Emily, but his hand irons rattled. Hobe quickly pulled away, ashamed.

"Hobe," said Pastor Henry, "we are here to support you and pray for you. I plan to speak to the judge on your behalf. Got some company with us." Henry pointed across the street. There were seven well-dressed young fellows coming his way. They were the orphans of Lubbock, but they didn't look like guttersnipes anymore.

"These are now our sons and Emily's brothers. We adopted them. The folks of Lubbock, the Christians of Lubbock, I should say, have pitched in to help us. You and Albert started all of this."

Levi stood next to Hobe and marveled at what he was hearing.

"We are not the only ones who have come to support you, Hobe. Look over yonder."

Hobe couldn't believe what he was seeing. There were some thirty people, including some of his family members, waving at him. "Don't think you're alone, Hobe. Whatever happens, we are here for you," said Henry. Sarah leaned over and kissed him on the cheek.

Emily ran over and hugged his leg. "I love you, Hobe."

He gently patted her on the head. "I love you too, Emily."

As Hobe stepped into the jail, with Levi behind him, he smiled and waved at his friends. Then he turned and saw Lucas reading from a piece of paper. From the marshal's somber expression and Rachael standing beside him, wiping tears from her eyes, Hobe knew the words on that paper spelled his doom.

"Hobe," said Lucas, "I've got some good news and some bad news for you."

"Well," said Hobe, "I could sure use some good news."

Lucas brushed the paper with his hand. "The judge has granted a stay of execution. You will not hang."

"That is good news," Hobe said with a big smile. "What's the bad news?"

Lucas looked down at the floor then back up at him. "You'll spend the rest of your life in the Leavenworth Territorial Prison."

Surprisingly, Hobe didn't flinch, nor did he panic. In fact, he smiled and said, "Well, I reckon I could have saved you a trip, Marshal. We rode right by there the other day." Rachel wept. "Those tears for me, Mrs. Rachael? I don't deserve them. I did wrong and now I have to pay for it."

Within a half hour, the news spread throughout the town of Caldwell. People gathered at the door of the jail to speak with Lucas. The strangers in town all turned out to be friends of Hobe and Albert—people who had benefited from meeting the Lett brothers. They were there as character references and wanted to know who they could speak with about lessening Hobe's sentence.

Lucas quickly sent for Hobe's lawyer. He told the people at his door that he was of the same mind as them. "Folks, now listen to me. We all know that Hobe Lett is a fine young man. He's made some bad choices, but I believe, like you do, that he needs to be given a second chance. Let's see what his lawyer says we can do, and then we'll get to doing it. Good enough?"

The crowd agreed and dispersed, only to come back the next morning. They were friendly and cordial, but quite concerned about Hobe being sent off to prison for life. A petition began to circulate. Pastor Henry Taylor and Pastor Jarvis Doran joined forces to pray and plan. They put together a letter with over one hundred signatures of people Albert and Hobe had helped, and sent it directly to the governor by train.

The night before Hobe was to leave Caldwell for the prison, a strange and angelic sound began resonating from his cell. With his beautiful tenor voice, Hobe Lett began to sing "Amazing Grace." He sang it as if God himself was sitting there on Hobe's bunk. The young man, whose heart had become hard as granite toward the things of God, had come back to his Lord. As a child growing up in a Christian home, he had sung beautiful Christian hymns. Many times, as the morning broke, Hobe's parents lay in their bed, hearing their little boy belting out the spirituals from his bed. It was always a blessing to them. Now, from a prison cell in Caldwell, Kansas, his singing wafted out of the cell window and into the streets like the sweet aroma of a freshly baked pie. The people on the boardwalks stopped and listened, and many of them worshipped the God Hobe sang about. His voice and the words he sang pierced their hearts.

Hobe was locked away behind steel bars, but for the first time in a long time he was experiencing the joy and freedom he had once known in Christ. Hobe Lett had come home to his faith in God.

To his amazement, the people gathered outside his cell window that night and joined him in singing the hymns that were so precious to the believers. It seemed the whole town of Caldwell was in the streets this night, praying, singing, and some, weeping.

But as the Bible says, joy comes in the morning. At daybreak, Lucas saddled his horse and one for Hobe. He had orders to deliver his prisoner to Leavenworth, a ride he didn't want to take, a duty he didn't want to fulfill, but one that had to be done.

As the two men climbed aboard their mounts, Hobe asked Lucas if he could speak to the crowd. Lucas nodded and said, "I don't think they'll let us leave until you do, son."

"Obliged, Marshal." Hobe faced his supporters. "Folks, I don't have the words to tell you how much your being here means to me. Me and my brother, well, we thought we were doing right. Had us a lot of anger at religious folk built up. I know now that so much of what we did was wrong down in here." Hobe pointed to his chest. "In the back of my mind, reckon I always knew it was wrong. But me and the Lord have things worked out now. I'm sorry, and I'm forgiven. Now, I got to take this ride, and I don't look forward to it. But the good Lord is going with me, and Marshal Reese."

"So are we!" hollered someone in the crowd. "Get your horses and your wagons. We're going to give Hobe an escort out of town."

Hobe looked at Lucas and shrugged his shoulders. "Don't rightly know what to make of this."

"Reckon it means they like you, Hobe," said Levi, standing next to Rachael. "And so do we." He leaned over and shook Hobe's hand.

Pastor Henry and Pastor Jarvis led the crowd down Main Street. They escorted Hobe three miles outside of town and stopped. Before the ministers could say anything, they heard thundering hooves. There was a cloud of dust coming their way from Caldwell. Lucas grabbed his field glasses and stuck them to his eyes. "It's John Riel. I ain't never seen him run so fast, especially on that jughead he rides."

John was another of Lucas' deputies. He was riding hard, waving a piece of paper, and yelling something that was difficult to understand. "What's he saying?" asked someone in the crowd.

As he got closer, the word "amnesty" was heard. "Amnesty! Amnesty, I tell you!" hollered John. He rode up and handed Lucas the telegram. "The governor has issued a pardon to Hobe Lett!" yelled Riel. Lucas nodded, confirming John's proclamation.

Cheers erupted from the bevy of folks surrounding Hobe and the lawmen. "Praise God from Whom all blessings flow!" exclaimed Pastor Jarvis.

Selah, Hobe's mother, ran to her son. Hobe stepped down off his horse and hugged his mother as he whispered in her ear. "It's a miracle, Ma. It's a miracle." They both cried tears of joy.

So is the story of the broken halo of Hobe Lett, a young boy whose heart was once tender toward God, but then became as hard as granite. A young boy, taught by his godly parents to love the Lord and people, but through some unfortunate experiences he turned against both. But now, through God's grace and the second chances He gives people, Hobe Lett was reclaimed and redeemed.

Hobe's story does not end there. Hobe stayed in Caldwell, Kansas and soon answered the call to be the worship pastor of Jarvis Doran's church, Caldwell Pointe. He married Rebekah, the beautiful, brown-eyed daughter of Marshal

Lucas and Rachael Reese. It was a cold December afternoon, the fourteenth, to be exact, when the two wed. There were three ministers present to officiate: Pastor Henry Taylor, Pastor Jarvis Doran, and Reverend Elvin Lett, Hobe's grandfather. Selah and Julie, along with her daughter, Danielle, and Julie's husband, were there as well.

What a celebration it was! Six months after Hobe's pardon, his life had changed drastically. He married a beautiful young Christian woman and committed his life to God's service. Dan would have been proud of his son. Selah told Hobe that, many times after his pardon. Ten months after Rebekah and Hobe married, they had a son. The name they gave him was Dan Albert Lett. They called him Little Dan, a fitting tribute to Hobe's father.

Hobe became a powerful influence in the town of Caldwell through his ministry at Caldwell Pointe. He often told people that if God could have mercy on Hobe Lett, a man who took the things of God and made a mockery out of them, then he would surely have mercy on anybody. Hobe was another trophy of God's grace shining brightly in Caldwell, Kansas. From Rachael being a saloon girl and cheating men out of their money, to Jarvis, her father, being a drunk and abandoning his children, and now, Hobe, a man sentenced to life in prison, God was putting trophies of His grace on display in Caldwell for all the West to see.

The End

About
Jim Burnett

Jim Burnett is a speaker and author who has pastored four churches in Mississippi in his thirty years in ministry. He has published a plethora of leadership articles for Christian magazines and has also written three Christian western series called Miracle at Caller's Spring Ranch, Jedidiah Justice. Currently there are five books in the Caller's Spring series and a sixth about to be released. His three bounty hunter novels include book one, "Relentless Justice," book two, "Persistent Justice, and book three, "Perpetual Justice."

He has a 15-book micro series out now titled, "Justice on the Frontier", which chronicles the exploits of Jedidiah Justice, Bounty Hunter of the Badlands.

As an advocate for prayer in public schools, Jim was interviewed on Fox and Friends. An avid horseman, he has a deep love for western heritage. He and his wife Kim have three children and three grandchildren.

Jim loves horses and has all of his life. He never imagined God using this affinity for ministry. He refers to his Christian western novels as "the gospel in a cowboy wrapper".

Mr. Burnett has a Bachelor of Science in Business Administration Degree from the University of Southern Mississippi and a Master of Divinity degree and Doctor of Ministry degree from the New Orleans Baptist Theological Seminary.

Printed in Great Britain
by Amazon